The Story of
of
DOG'S EYE

Mohamed Fayaz

The Story of DOG'S EYE
Copyright © 2024 Mohamed Fayaz

ISBN: 978-93-6249-820-5
Publishing Year 2024

Published by:
Dreambook Publishing
Phone: +917249951871
Email: info@dreambookpublishing.com
Website: www.dreambookpublishing.com

Preface

In a world where the line between life and death is often drawn with sharp clarity, there are moments when that boundary blurs, and the past refuses to rest.

"The Story of Dog's Eye" is a fictional story that deals into the life of Mohan, a man whose duties as a police officer bring him face to face with the consequences of a single, fateful accident. What begins as a routine investigation quickly spirals into a harrowing encounter with the supernatural, where guilt, deception, and vengeance merge into a chilling quest for redemption.

After surviving a horrific crash that leaves him scarred, Mohan unknowingly becomes the target of a vengeful spirit. The ghost, driven by deep resentment, weaves a sinister plot that devastates Mohan's life, turning him against those he loves most. Blinded by fabricated evidence and misled by an unseen force, Mohan loses his family's love and respect, his peace, and his faith.

This tale, blending elements of conflicts, sentiments, along with thriller, horror, suspense and spiritual reflection, invites readers into a world where the natural and supernatural collide, where the weight of unspoken sins can echo across lifetimes, and where the power of forgiveness may be the only way to escape the chains of the past.

Contents

CHAPTER 1

The jungle was dark and full of the sounds of the night. Crickets were chirping, and every now and then, an owl was hooting from somewhere deep within the trees. The air was heavy with moisture, smelling of wet leaves and damp earth. A narrow dirt road wound through the thick forest, barely visible under the dim light ofthe moon.

A jeep was driving along this road, its headlights shining through the darkness. Inside the jeep was a police officer, a man used to tough situations. Beside him sat his loyal pet dog, a strong and brave companion who had been by his side for years. The officer was focused on the rough road ahead, knowing that the jungle could be unpredictable, especially at night.

But far ahead, another set of headlights appeared, swerving wildly on the narrow road. It was a car, speeding through the jungle as if the driver was lost and scared. The car was coming too fast for the bumpy, uneven road, and the driver was having trouble controlling it.

Suddenly, at a sharp bend in the road, the car and the jeep came face to face. The road was too narrow, and there wasn't enough time to stop. The police officer quickly tried to steer the jeep out of the way, but the car was already too close.With a loud crash, the car slammed into the sideof the jeep. Metal crunched and twisted as both vehicles were thrown off the road into the thick bushes and trees.

Inside the jeep, the police officer was thrown forward, hitting his head against the steering wheel. The jeep tipped over onto its side, and the officer felt a sharp pain in his head and leg.The world around him spun as he tried to understand what had happened. His ears rang from the noise of the crash, and his vision was blurry.

He tried to stay awake, to fight the encroaching blackness, but it was no use. The last thing he remembered before everything went dark was the still form of his dog, lying motionless outside the jeep, and the unbearable grief that gripped hisheart.

Time passed in a haze. There were moments of fleeting awareness—flashes of light, the muffled sound of voices, the sensation of being lifted and carried—but they all felt like fragments of a distant dream, he was slipping deeper into unconsciousness.

When he finally awoke, it was to a dim light that felt far gentler than the harsh glare of the jeep's head lights. The air was different; it was no longer heavy with the scent of moisture soaked earth and crushed leaves, but cleaner, with the faint antiseptic smell of a hospital. Slowly, painfully, the officer opened his eyes. His left eye fluttered open, revealing the unfamiliar surroundings of a small, modest hospital room. But his right eye refused to obey. Panic surged through him as he instinctively reached up to touch his face. His fingers brushed against something soft and thick—a bandage wrapped tightly around his head, covering his right eye.

He tried to sit up, but a sharp pain shot through his body, forcing him back down. It was then that the memories of the accident came rushing back—the blinding headlights, the screech of tires, the violent impact that had thrown him and his dog into the unforgiving jungle. And then, the terrible realization hit him like a blow: his dog!

Frantically, he looked around the small room, searching for any sign of his loyal companion. But the room was empty, save for the quiet hum of medical equipment and the occasional rustle of a nurse passing by in the hallway. His heart pounded in his chest as he struggled to breathe, his mind racing with fear and sorrow.

A soft knock on the door pulled him from his thoughts, and a nurse stepped in, her face kind but serious. She approached the officer's bedside, placing a gentle hand on his arm to calm him. "You're awake," she said softly. "How are you feeling?" The officer's voice was hoarse and weak as he asked the only question that mattered to him. "My dog... where's my dog?"

The nurse's expression faltered, a shadow of sadness passing over her face. She hesitated for a moment, and in that moment, the officer knew. His heart sank, the weight of loss pressing down on him like a heavy stone.

"I'm so sorry," the nurse said quietly. "Your dog… he didn't make it. The impact was too severe."

The officer closed his eyes, fighting back the tears that threatened to spill over. His faithful companion, the one who had been with him through countless trials and dangers, was gone. The pain of that loss cut deeper than any of his physical injuries.

But there was more. The nurse took a deep breath, knowing she had to tell him the rest. "You were seriously injured in the accident," she continued gently. "You've lost vision in your right eye. The doctors did everything they could, but the damage was too extensive." The officer reached up again, his hand trembling as it touched the bandage over his eye. He felt a mix of disbelief and despair, struggling to process the reality of what had happened. His career, his life—it all felt so uncertain now, shadowed by the loss of his eye and the death of his beloved dog.

For a long time, he laid there in silence, the nurse quietly respecting his need for space. The jungle, which had seemed so full of life and sound the night before, now felt like a distant, hostile memory. He had survived, but at a great cost.

Finally, he opened his left eye again and looked at the nurse. "Where am I?" he asked, his voice barely above a whisper.

"You're in a small hospital near the jungle," she explained. "A rescue team found you and brought you here. You were lucky they arrived when they did. You're safe now, and we'll take care of you."

The officer nodded, though the word "lucky" felt strange to him. He couldn't shake the feeling of loss that weighed so heavily on his chest. But as he lay there, in the quiet of the hospital room, he knew that he had to find a way to move forward. His dog would want that—his brave companion wouldn't want him to give up.

The road to recovery would be long, and the wounds— both physical and emotional—would take time to heal. But for now, the officer allowed himself a moment of grief, closing his eye and letting the tears flow freely. He was alive, but he would never be the same.

News of the accident spread quickly. It wasn't long before a close friend of the police officer, another officer who had worked alongside him for years, heard what had happened. The moment the call came through, his heart sank. Without wasting a second, he jumped into his car and sped towards the small hospital near the jungle, where his friend had been taken.

When he arrived at the hospital, the sun was just beginning to rise, casting a pale light over the landscape. He parked haphazardly and rushed inside, his shoes squeaking on the wet floor as he hurried to the reception desk.

"Where is he?" he asked, breathless, barely able to keep the panic out of his voice. "The officer who was in the accident where is he?"

The receptionist, seeing the urgency in his eyes, quickly directed him to the right wing of the hospital. "He's in Room 12," she said. "But please, be prepared. He's been through a lot."

He nodded, swallowing the lump in his throat, and made his way down the quiet corridor. The hospital smelled of antiseptic, and the fluorescent lights cast a harsh glow on the pale walls. Each step felt heavier than the last, as if he was walking towards a reality he wasn't ready to face.

Finally, he reached Room 12. The door was slightly ajar, and through the crack, he could see his friend lying in the hospital bed, bandaged and still. For a moment, he just stood there, frozen by the sight of the man who had always been so strong, now looking so vulnerable. Taking a deep breath, he pushed the door open and stepped inside. The officer in the bed didn't stir—he was asleep, his chest rising and falling steadily, but his face was pale, and the bandage over his right eye was stark against his skin.

A doctor, who had been checking the monitors by the bed, turned to face the new comer. "Are you a friend?" the doctor asked softly, noticing the tension in the man's stance.

"Yes," he replied, his voice thick with emotion. "How is he? What's his condition?"

The doctor sighed, his expression compassionate yet grave. "He's stable now, but he's been through a lot. The accident was severe—he lost his right eye, and he has other injuries that will take time to heal. He's also dealing with significant emotional trauma, particularly from the loss of his dog."

The friend's shoulders slumped as the weight of the doctor's words hit him. He glanced at his unconscious friend, his heart aching for the pain and loss he must have endured. "Will he be okay?" he asked, though he wasn't sure what answer he was hoping for.

The doctor gave a small nod. "Physically, with time and care, he should recover. But emotionally, it's going to be a harder road. He'll need support—from friends like you. This kind of loss… it's not something you get over easily."

The friend nodded, determined. "He won't gothrough this alone. I'll be here for him, whatever he needs."

The doctor offered a reassuring smile. "That willmake all the difference."

They both fell silent, the beeping of the monitors and the faint hum of the hospital the only sounds in the room. The friend moved closer to the bed, pulling up a chair and sitting down beside his injured companion. He reachedout and gently placed a hand on his friend's arm, a silent promise that he would be there, no matter what.

As the hours passed, the friend stayed by the officer's side, keeping watch as his friend slept. He thought about the man he had known for so long—their shared experiences, the dangers they had faced together, and the unspoken bond that had formed between them. Seeing him like this was difficult, but it only strengthened his resolve to help him through the difficult days ahead.

The morning sun gradually brightened the room, casting soft light on the hospital bed. As the doctor finished checking the police officer's vitals, he turned to the friend who wassitting quietly by the bed. The doctor could see the concern etched on the man's face, and he knew that the story of the man lying unconscious before them must be one worth hearing.

"Your friend is fortunate to have someone like you by his side," the doctor began gently. "It's clear he's been through a lot, not just with the accident, but in life as well. Sometimes, knowing more about a patient's history can help us understand how to support them better in their recovery. Could you tell me more about him? His name, his life before all this?"

The friend nodded slowly, his eyes still fixed on the injured officer. "His name is Mohan Kumar," he began, his voice low and reflective. "He's always been a fighter, even from a young age.

He grew up in Mangalore, a bustling city by the sea. But life wasn't easy for him. He lost his father when he was just a child, and from that moment on, he had to grow up fast."

The doctor listened intently, sensing that this was a story filled with both pain and perseverance.

"Mohan's mother, Kamala Devi, was a strong woman," the friend continued. "She did everything she could to raise him on her own. They didn't have much, but she worked hard, taking on odd jobs to make sure there was food on the table and that Mohan could go to school. She was his anchor, the one person who always believed in him, no matter how tough things got."

The friend paused, memories flooding back as he spoke. "But Mohan was determined, even as a boy. He knew that if he wanted to change his life, he had to work for it. He was always at the top of his class, but it wasn't just about the grades for him. He wanted to prove that he could rise above the circumstances he was born into." The doctor nodded, appreciating the strength it must have taken for Mohan to come as far as he had. "It sounds like he's had to overcome a lot," the doctor said softly.

"He has," the friend agreed. "Mohan never let anything stand in his way. After school, he joined the police academy. It wasn't easy, especially without a father to guide him, but he pushed through. He used to tell me that he wanted to protect others, to be the kind of person who could make a difference. And that's   exactly what he did.

He worked his way up through the ranks, earning the respect of everyone around him."

The friend's expression softened as he spoke about the happier moments in Mohan's life. "A few years ago, he married Geetha, a wonderful woman who understood his commitment to hiswork. They were a perfect match—both strong, both determined to make a better life for themselves. Geetha brought joy into his life, a sense of completeness that he hadn't felt since he was a child. "The doctor could see the admiration in the friend's eyes as he spoke about Mohan's journey. "He must be a remarkable man," thedoctor said.

"He is," the friend replied, his voice thick with emotion. "But he's also human. Life hasn't been kind to him, and even with all his strength, there are scars that run deep. This accident… losing his dog, his eye… it's going to be another battle for him. But if there's one thing I know about Mohan, it's that he won't give up. He's fought too hard to let this break him."

The room fell into a contemplative silence. The doctor could see that Mohan's past had shaped him into the resilient, determined man lying before them. Yet, he also understood that this latest trauma would require all the support andstrength his friend and loved ones could offer.

"You've given me a clear picture of who he is," the doctor finally said, his voice filled with respect. "We'll do everything we can to help himthrough this. But he's going to need you, and his family, more than ever now."

The friend nodded, resolute. "I'll be here, and so will his family. Mohan's been there for all of uswhen we needed him. Now it's our turn to be there for him."

As the doctor quietly left the room, the friend remained by Mohan's side, his mind swirling with memories of their past together and the uncertain future that now lay ahead. He knew that the road to recovery would be long and difficult, but he was determined to walk it with his friend, every step of the way.

CHAPTER 2

The friend sat in silence, watching over Mohan as memories of their shared past played out in his mind. The bond between Mohan and his pet dog had always been something special, a connection that went beyond the ordinary relationship between a man and his pet.

The doctor returned quietly, holding a clipboard but with an expression of gentle curiosity. He noticed the distant look in the friend's eyes, and after a moment, he spoke softly, "I've heard a bit about Mohan's life, but I'd also like to know about his dog. The friend's gaze softened, and a sad smile crossed his face as he recalled the story of how Mohan and his dog had found each other. "That dog… it wasn't just any dog. It wasn't a purebred or something fancy. In fact, it was just a street dog, a stray. But to Mohan, it was everything."

The doctor pulled up a chair and sat down, sensing there was a story here worth hearing.

The friend began, his voice tinged with nostalgia. "It was a few years ago, on one of Mohan's late-night patrols. He was driving through a rough part of the city when he saw something on the side of the road. At first, he thought it was just some trash or debris, but then he noticed it moves. It was a small dog, thin and battered, barely more than a puppy. Someone had hit it with a car and just left itthere to die."

The doctor's expression tightened as he listened, and the friend continued. "Mohan couldn't just drive by and ignore it. He pulled over, picked up the little thing, and took it to a nearby vet. The dog was in bad shape, but somehow, it pulled through. Mohan decided right then that he couldn't leave it behind. He brought it home, nursed it back to health, and from that day on, they were inseparable."

The friend paused, a fond smile touching his lips as he remembered how the scrappy little dog had changed Mohan's life. "Mohan named him Tiger, even though he was small and scruffy. But that name fit him in spirit. He had the heart of a lion, that dog. He was fiercely loyal, and despite everything he'd been through, he was always full of energy and love."

The doctor nodded, picturing the scene in his mind. "It sounds like they saved each other," heobserved.

"They did," the friend agreed. "You see, Mohan wasn't just saving the dog that night—Tiger was saving him too. Mohan had always been a strong man, but he carried a lot of weight on his shoulders. The stress of the job, the memories ofhis difficult childhood… they never really left him. But with Tiger around, things were different. That little dog had a way of making the world seem a little less heavy."

The friend's eyes grew distant as he continued."There was one time, not long after Mohan brought Tiger home, when the dog returned the favor. Mohan was on an undercover operation, something dangerous. He didn't want to leave Tiger behind, so he took him along, thinking it would be safer than leaving him home alone.

They were out in a remote area, similar to thatjungle road from last night."

The doctor leaned in slightly, intrigued bywhere the story was going.

"Mohan was staking out a location, watching for some criminals he'd been tracking for weeks. He was focused on the mission, but Tiger, with his sharp instincts, sensed something was off. Suddenly, Tiger started barking furiously. At first, Mohan tried to quiet him down, worried the barking would give them away. But Tiger wouldn't stop. Then, in the split second that followed, Mohan saw what Tiger had sensed—a shadow moving behind him."

The friend's voice grew tense, reliving the moment. "It was one of the criminals, sneakingup behind Mohan with a knife. If Tiger hadn't warned him… well, I'm not sure Mohan would be here today. Thanks to that dog's quick thinking, Mohan was able to defend himself andfinish the operation successfully. From that day on, their bond was something even deeper.

They trusted each other completely."

The doctor listened, clearly moved by the story. "It must have been incredibly hard for Mohan to lose his dog in the accident," he said softly.

The friend's eyes grew misty as he nodded. "Yes… losing Tiger was like losing a part of himself. That dog wasn't just a pet; he was family. They'd been through so much together, and Tiger had become Mohan's constant companion, his protector, and his confidant. Mohan's work was dangerous, but with Tiger by his side, he always felt a little safer, a little less alone."

The room fell silent as the weight of the loss settled over them both. The friend glanced at Mohan's still form, the bandages covering the wounds from the accident, and sighed deeply. "This isn't going to be easy for him," he murmured. "Mohan has lost a lot in his life, but this… this will be one of the hardest things he's ever faced."

The bond between Mohan and Tiger had been extraordinary, a connection forged in loyalty and love.

And though Tiger was gone, the friend believed that the little dog's spirit would continue to watch over Mohan, guiding him through the darkness until he found the light again.

As the hours ticked by, the small hospital room remained a quiet sanctuary for Mohan, who still lay unconscious, recovering from the accident. The friend kept vigil by his side, lost in thought, until the soft creak of the door broke the silence.

A young police constable stepped into the room. His face was a mixture of concern and exhaustion, but his eyes lit up with relief when he saw Mohan lying in the bed, bandaged but alive. The constable's presence brought a new sense of tension into the room. The doctor, who had been reviewing Mohan's charts, looked up at the new arrival with a polite nod. "Are you here to see the officer?" he asked, glancing between the constable and Mohan's friend.

"Yes, sir," the constable replied, his voice soft but earnest. "Mohan is my cousin."

The doctor's eyebrows lifted in mild surprise. "I see. You're family, then?"

The friend, who had been watching the exchange in silence, smiled warmly at the constable. "Yes, Doctor. They're cousins, but it'smore than just blood that ties them together.

They've always had a close bond, almost likebrothers."

The constable stepped closer to the bed, his gaze fixed on Mohan's still form. "Mohan was always there for me," he began, his voice thick with emotion. "When I was a kid, my father passed away suddenly, and my mother was struggling to raise us on her own. Mohan, even though he was young himself, took me under his wing. He taught me everything—how to be strong, how to fight for what's right."

The doctor listened with quiet attentiveness, sensing the deep connection between the two men. "It sounds like Mohan has been an important figure in your life."

The constable nodded, his eyes never leaving Mohan. "He has, Doctor. He's more than just a cousin to me. He's my mentor, my guide .Everything I've done, everything I've become, it's because of him. When I decided to join the police force, it was because I wanted to be likeMohan. He showed me what it means to serve and protect, not just with words, but throughhis actions."

The friend, watching the constable's emotional expression, added, "Mohan always believed in looking out for family. After he lost his father, he made it his mission to take care of those around him. Whether it was his mother, his wife, or his cousin here, Mohan always made sure they were safe and taken care of. He's got a big heart, even though he doesn't always show it."

The constable's voice trembled slightly as he continued, "When I joined the force, Mohan took it upon himself to guide me through every step. He was hard on me, made sure I knew what I was getting into. But that's just how he is—tough love, you know? He wanted to make sure I was ready, that I could handle the pressures of the job. And I'll tell you, Doctor, he's the reason I've made it this far."

The doctor observed the deep respect and love in the constable's voice, understanding more about Mohan with every word. "He must be very proud of you," the doctor said gently.

The constable swallowed hard, his eyes glistening. "I hope so. I've always tried to live up to his example. And now… seeing him like this, knowing what he's been through… it's hard. It's hard to see someone so strong, someone you look up to, lying there, hurt and vulnerable."

The friend placed a reassuring hand on the constable's shoulder. "Mohan's a fighter. He's been through worse, and he's come out stronger each time. He'll get through this, too. But he'll need us—both of us—to be there for him, just like he's always been there for us."The constable nodded his resolve firming up. "Whatever he needs, I'll be here. I owe him that much, and so much more."

The doctor, moved by the loyalty and love that surrounded Mohan, spoke with a calm assurance. "With support like this, Mohan will have every chance to heal, not just physically, but emotionally as well. It's clear he's made a difference in many lives, and now it's time for those lives to support him in return."

The three men—Mohan's friend, his cousin, and the doctor—shared a moment of understanding. Each of them knew that the road to recovery would be long and challenging, but they also knew that with the strength of family and friendship, Mohan wouldn't have to walk that road alone.

CHAPTER 3

As the constable settled into the chair beside Mohan's bed, a new commotion erupted in the hallway outside. The sound of hurried footsteps, mingled with sobs and frantic voices, grew louder as two women rushed toward the room, their cries of anguish echoing down the corridor.

The door burst open, and in came an elderly woman with silver-streaked hair, her face etched with deep lines of worry. She was followed closely by a younger woman, her eyesred and swollen from tears, her hands trembling as she clutched a small handbag to her chest.

"Mohan!" the older woman cried out, her voice breaking as she saw her son lying unconscious in the hospital bed. "My son, my son!" Her hands shook as she reached out, as if trying to bridge the distance between them through sheer will alone. The younger woman, her tears flowing freely, moved to the other side of the bed, gently touching Mohan's hand as if her touch might wake him from his deep slumber. "Please, Mohan, open your eyes," she whispered, her voice choked with emotion. "You can't leave us like this."

Mohan's friend quickly rose from his seat, his heart aching at the sight of the two women he knew so well— Kamala Devi, Mohan's mother, and Geetha, his beloved wife. The doctor, observing the scene, glanced at the friend, who nodded in understanding.

"These are Mohan's mother and wife," the friend said quietly, his voice filled with sympathy. "They're everything to him, and he's everything to them."

The doctor nodded, recognizing the depth of the bond between the women and the man lying in the bed. "Tell me more about them," he requested gently, understanding that knowing more about Mohan's family would help him understand his patient better.

The friend sighed deeply, looking at the two women who were now seated on either side of Mohan, each of them holding onto him as if he were their lifeline. "Kamala Devi… she's a remarkable woman. She raised Mohan on her own after his father passed away when Mohan was just a boy. Life wasn't easy for her, but she never gave up. She worked day and night, taking on any job she could find, just to make sure Mohan had a roof over his head and food on the table."

The friend's voice softened with admiration. "She taught Mohan the values of hard work and resilience. Even when times were tough, she always believed that he could achieve great things. And he did. It's because of her that Mohan became the man he is today—a man of integrity, strength, and deep compassion."

The doctor glanced at Kamala Devi, her grief- stricken face now resting against Mohan's hand, and he could see the strength in her, even in this moment of vulnerability. She was a woman who had faced countless challenges, and yet, her love for her son had always been unwavering.

"And Geetha," the friend continued, his gaze shifting to the younger woman, "she's been Mohan's rock. They met in Mangalore, and from the moment they met, Mohan knew she was theone for him.

Geetha comes from a humble background, but she has a heart of gold. She's stood by Mohan through everything—his demanding job, the long nights, the dangers he faced as a police officer. She never once complained. Instead, she became his source of strength, always supporting him, alwaysbelieving in him."

The friend's voice grew softer, filled with emotion. "Mohan and Geetha share a love that'struly special. They don't need to say much to each other—they just understand. They've been through so much together, and Geetha has always been his safe harbor. When Mohan comes home after a long day, it's Geetha who makes everything right again."

The doctor watched as Geetha leaned in closer to Mohan, her fingers brushing a stray lock of hair from his forehead. Despite the tears streaming down her face, there was a tenderness in her touch, a quiet strength that spoke volumes about the depth of their relationship.

"Mohan is a lucky man to have these women in his life," the doctor remarked, his voice full of respect. "It's clear they mean the world to him."

The friend nodded, his heart heavy with the weight of the moment. "Yes, Doctor. They've been his foundation, his reason for fighting through every challenge. And now, they're theones who will help him through this."

As the friend spoke, Kamala Devi looked up, hereyes filled with a mother's fierce love. "My son is strong," she said, her voice trembling but resolute. "He's always been a fighter. And with Geetha and me by his side, he will overcome this too."

Geetha, still holding Mohan's hand, nodded in agreement. "We won't leave him, not for a moment. We'll be here, waiting for him to wake up, to see us again. He's always been there for us, and now it's our turn to be there for him."

In that small hospital room, surrounded by those who loved him most, Mohan's journey to recovery had truly begun—not just with the healing of his body, but with the unwavering support of the two women who had shaped his life and held his heart.

As the doctor listened to the heartfelt stories about Mohan's family, he found himself drawn into the intricate web of relationships that surrounded the injured officer. Yet, there was one story still untold, one that might provide the final piece to understanding the man before him.

The doctor glanced at Mohan's friend, who had been the anchor of calm throughout this emotional storm. "You've shared so much about Mohan's family," the doctor began gently, "but what about you? You clearly care a great deal for him. How did you two become friends?"

The friend, who had been standing quietly by the window, turned to face the doctor. A soft, reminiscent smile appeared on his face as he considered the question. "My name is Ramesh," he said, his voice warm with the familiarity of a long-shared bond. "Mohan and I have known each other for as long as I can remember."

Ramesh took a deep breath, his eyes distant as memories flooded back. "We grew up in the same neighborhood in Mangalore. Back then, we were just a couple of kids running around the streets, getting into all sorts of trouble. Mohan was always the leader—brave, determined, always ready to stand up for what he believed in. Even as a boy, he had this sense of justice that set him apart."

The doctor nodded, intrigued by this glimpse into Mohan's early life. "It sounds like you've been through a lot together."

Ramesh chuckled softly. "That's an understatement. We were inseparable. When Mohan's father passed away, I saw how much it affected him. He was just a kid, but he suddenly had all this responsibility thrust upon him. I tried to be there for him as much as I could. We spent countless hours together, talking about our dreams, our fears, and what we wanted to do with our lives."

He paused, his voice taking on a more serious tone. "Mohan always knew he wanted to make a difference. He talked about becoming a police officer even back then. It wasn't just a job to him—it was a calling. And when he set his mind to something, there was no stopping him. I knew he would achieve his dream, no matter what it took."

The doctor looked at Ramesh with newfound respect. "It sounds like your friendship has been a cornerstone in both your lives."

Ramesh nodded. "It has been. Mohan is more than just a friend to me—he's like a brother. We've seen each other through the worst of times and celebrated the best of them. And now, seeing him like this, it's hard, Doctor. It's really hard. But I know Mohan, and I know he's a fighter. He's not going to let this beat him."

The doctor offered a reassuring smile. "With friends like you by his side, I'm sure he'll pull through. You've been a great support to him, Ramesh, and that's something no amount of medicine can replace."

Ramesh returned the smile, though his eyes were still shadowed with worry. "I'll be here for him, just like he's always been there for me. Whatever it takes, I'll do it. Mohan has always been there to catch me when I fell, and now it's my turn to do the same for him."

The room, once filled with grief and uncertainty, now hummed with a quiet, steadfast resolve.

The stories of friendship, family, and loyalty had painted a vivid picture of who Mohan Kumar was—not just a police officer, but a man deeply loved and respected by those who knew him best.

Ramesh, still reflecting on the deep bond he shared with Mohan, turned back to the doctor, who seemed curious. "So, Ramesh, what is your profession? You mentioned that Mohan always stood by you, even when life took different directions. What path did you end up following?"

Ramesh smiled faintly. "I'm a police officer too, just like Mohan. He inspired me to take up the badge. I suppose you could say I'm following in his footsteps, though I've never quite lived up to the man he is."

Before the doctor could respond, the peaceful atmosphere in the room was shattered by a sudden, agonizing scream. Mohan, lying on the hospital bed, began thrashing, his face contorted in pain. Blood started pouring from his right eye, staining the bandages and the pillow beneath his head.

Kamala Devi gasped, clutching her chest in horror, while Geetha screamed, "Mohan! What's happening?" Ramesh rushed to his friend's side, his heart pounding in his chest as he saw the crimson trail running down Mohan's face.

The doctor sprang into action, pushing everyone back to give him space. "We need to act fast!" he barked, his calm demeanor replaced by the urgency of the situation. He quickly examined Mohan's eye, his expression growing graver by the second. "The blood isn't stopping. We need to perform immediate surgery, or he could lose more than just his eye. "Panic gripped the room, but Ramesh, despite hisfear, asked, "Is there anything we can do?

Anything at all?"

The doctor's face was set in concentration, his mind racing as he considered their limited options. "We don't have the proper surgical facilities here," he admitted, his voice strained. "This hospital isn't equipped for complex procedures like eye surgery, but I have to stop the bleeding and stabilize him somehow. If we don't act now, we'll lose him."

Geetha sobbed quietly, clutching her mother-in-law as they both watched helplessly. Ramesh stood frozen, desperate for a solution, when suddenly the doctor's eyes flickered with a strange idea—one that was as unorthodox as it was desperate.

"Mohan's dog," the doctor murmured, almost tohimself. He looked up at the family, his face a mix of determination and uncertainty. "I know this sounds unusual, but I might be able to save his eye using a technique I've read about in emergency field medicine. It involves transplanting tissue from another source—in this case, the dog's eye."

The room fell silent as the weight of his words sank in. Kamala Devi and Geetha stared at the doctor in shock, while Ramesh, still trying to process what was happening, found his voice. "Are you saying… you want to use the dog's eye to replace Mohan's?"

The doctor nodded, his expression serious. "It's a risky procedure, and I've never done anythinglike it before. But Mohan's dog—it died in the accident, didn't it? We could potentially use the eye tissue to stabilize the damage and buy us time until we can get him to a better-equipped facility."

Geetha, still trembling, looked at Ramesh for guidance. "Would it even work? Could this savehim?"

The doctor sighed, knowing the enormity of what he was suggesting. "There's no guarantee, but it might stop the bleeding and save his life. I'll need your permission to proceed."

Kamala Devi, her heart breaking at the thought of losing her son, nodded slowly. "If there's evena chance… If it can help my boy… then do it, Doctor. Do whatever you have to."

Ramesh, though stunned by the idea, knew that time was running out. "Mohan loved that dog like it was family. If there's a chance it could save him… then we have to try."

With the family's consent, the doctor rushed to prepare for the procedure, his mind focused on the daunting task ahead. The small hospital's staff scrambled to assist, bringing whatever tools they had at their disposal. The doctor worked with meticulous care, knowing that any mistake could cost Mohan's life.

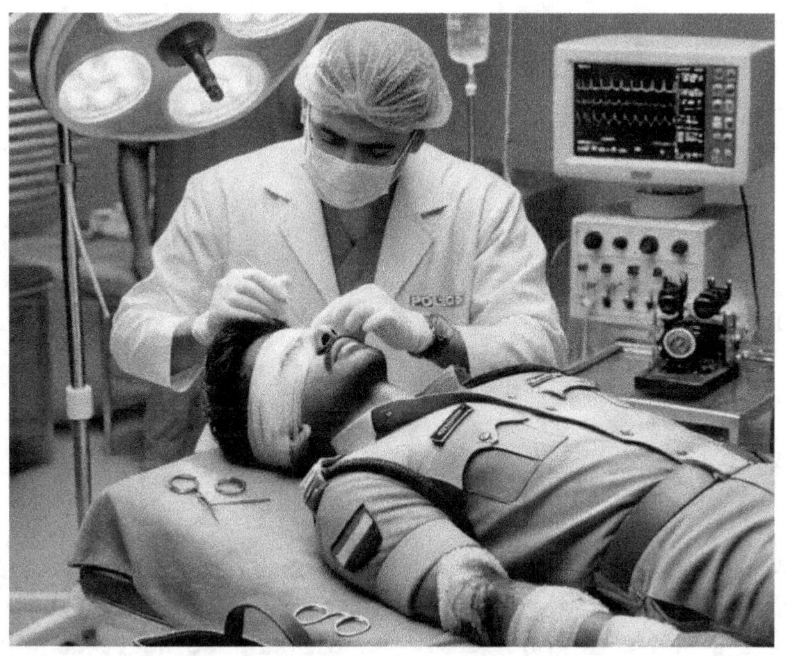

Hours passed, each moment filled with tension and hope as the doctor performed the makeshift surgery. Ramesh, Kamala Devi, and Geetha waited in the hallway, their hearts heavy with fear and anticipation. The silence was oppressive, broken only by the soft hum of the hospital's machinery and the occasional footstep echoing in the distance.

Finally, the doctor emerged, his face lined with exhaustion but his eyes holding a glimmer of hope. "The surgery is done," he announced. "I've managed to stabilize him using the dog's eye tissue. It's not a perfect solution, but it stopped the bleeding. Mohan is strong, and he's holding on."

Relief washed over them, though it was tinged with the sobering realization of what had just occurred. Kamala Devi whispered a prayer of thanks, while Geetha's tears flowed freely, a mix of sorrow and hope.

Ramesh, though relieved, couldn't help but marvel at the strange twist of fate that had ledto this moment. "Mohan's dog saved him… evenin death," he murmured, his voice filled with emotion. "That dog was always protecting him, and now… it's a part of him."

The doctor nodded, understanding the profound bond that had been honored in that operating room. "Yes, it seems the dog's loyalty extends beyond life itself. Mohan still has a long road ahead, but this was the first step in that journey."

As the night stretched on, the family and Ramesh remained by Mohan's side, watchingover him as he rested.

And as the first rays of sunlight began to filter through the trees, casting a gentle glow over the small hospital, there was a sense of renewed hope. Mohan had survived the night, thanks to the combined strength of his family, his friend, and the unwavering bond with his loyal companion—a bond that had transcended even death to give him another chance at life.

CHAPTER 4

Mohan sat alone in the small, dimly lit police station, surrounded by the quiet hum of paperwork and the distant sound of traffic. The rain outside pattered softly against the windows, a constant reminder of the night that had changed everything. He leaned back in his chair, staring blankly at the stack of files before him, his once proud uniform replaced by a simple shirt and tie, marking his new role as a clerk. The weight of disappointment pressed heavily on his chest.

He was no longer the officer who had once roamed the streets, chasing down criminals, solving cases, and upholding the law with courage and conviction. His right eye—now replaced with the eye of his loyal dog—could no longer see, leaving him reliant on his left. The demotion had come swiftly after his recovery, a blow to his pride that hurt more than the physical wounds. The police force he had dedicated his life to had deemed him unfit for duty. They gave him a desk job, and with that, the essence of who he was seemed to fade away.

Mohan glanced around the small station, its walls filled with reminders of the job he loved and had lost. His fingers absently touched the patch of cloth tied over his right eye, a constant reminder of what had been taken from him. The sight from his left eye was clear, but it wasn't the same. It was like seeing the world through a distorted lens—one half of him alive and alert, the other shrouded in darkness and memories.

He slowly turned his chair to face the small, cracked mirror hanging on the wall beside his desk. His reflection stared back at him—hollow, tired, and broken. His face, once marked by strength and purpose, was now overshadowed by the cloth covering his right eye. Beneath the cloth, the dog's eye—his dog's eye—remained hidden, a permanent reminder of the life he had lost in that jungle. Every time he thought of it, his heart clenched with sorrow.

In that reflective moment, he saw not only his own face but the face of the dog that had given everything for him. His loyal companion had saved his life, and now, even in death, the dog was still a part of him. But it wasn't a comfort. Instead, it was a cruel reminder of all he had lost—the faithful friend who had died in his arms, the eye that was no longer his own, and the career that had been ripped away from him. The jungle, the crash, the blood, and the storm all came rushing back to him like a nightmare that refused to fade.

Mohan covered his right eye with his hand, as if hiding it from the world, trying to erase the painful memories. But they were too strong, too deeply etched into his soul. He could hear the dog's bark, see the fear in its eyes as the accident unfolded, and feel the cold weight of the loss that followed.

"Why did it have to end like this?" Mohan whispered to himself, his voice thick with frustration. He had worked so hard to get to where he was, overcoming the hardships of his childhood, rising through the ranks with sheer determination. And now, all of that seemed like a distant dream, slipping further away with each passing day. He felt like a shadow of the man he once was.

He took a deep breath, trying to steady his emotions, but the bitterness remained. How could he go on like this? A once proud police officer, reduced to clerical work, a man who could no longer face danger because he had already been defeated by it. His right hand clenched into a fist as the pain of his demotion, of losing his beloved dog, and of losing his eye all collided within him.

Mohan leaned forward, covering his face with his hands, as if trying to shut out the world and everything he had lost. The sound of the storm outside mirrored the storm within him. He didn't know how to move forward, how to live with the eye that wasn't his, how to live with the knowledge that his dog had sacrificed itself for him. He didn't know how to live without the uniform he had worn with pride.

But as he sat there, he also realized something. His dog, even in death, had saved his life. He was still alive. He had a chance to figure out what came next, even if it wasn't the life he had imagined. The road ahead was uncertain and painful, but maybe, just maybe, he could find a way to honour the sacrifices that had been made.

With a heavy sigh, Mohan slowly tied the cloth tighter over his right eye, concealing the part of him that now carried the dog's essence. He stood up, feeling the weight of his past, yet knowing he still had a future to face, no matter how uncertain it seemed.

Mohan stepped out of the police station into the stormy night. The wind howled through the empty streets, and sheets of rain fell relentlessly from the dark sky. It was nearly midnight, and the world around him seemed to disappear into the shadows. The streetlights flickered weakly, barely cutting through the thick curtain of rain, and the only sounds were the distant rumble of thunder and the rush of water running along the gutters.

He stood under the small awning in front of the station, waiting for his friend who had promised to pick him up. The cold wind bit at his skin, sending a shiver through his bones. The night felt heavy, filled with an unsettling energy that made the hair on the back of his neck stand up. As the minutes ticked by, Mohan realized that his friend wasn't coming. The storm had worsened, and perhaps the roads were flooded or the weather too dangerous for travel.

With a sigh, Mohan decided to walk home. He waited for the rain to ease, and when it finally did, he stepped out into the quiet, deserted street. The wind still whipped around him, and the cloth tied over his right eye flapped lightly with each gust. His left eye, the one that had remained untouched, scanned the streets ahead, but it was his right eye—the one that held the essence of his dog—that suddenly stirred to life.

At first, it was just a flicker, a blur of movement that seemed out of place in the corner of his vision. Mohan paused, his heart skipping a beat as he glanced to his right, where his vision was supposed to be dark. But to his shock, he saw something— something moving in the distance.

Through the shaking cloth, he caught a glimpse of figures— shadowy, indistinct, and moving strangely under the flickering streetlights. They weren't walking like normal people; their movements were jerky, almost unnatural, as if they were gliding through the storm rather than walking through it. Mohan blinked, convinced that it was his mind playing tricks on him. He knew he shouldn't be able to see from that eye. After all, it wasn't his own.

But as he adjusted the cloth, pulling it away slightly to clear his vision, the figures became clearer. They were real—pale, ghostly figures, moving aimlessly through the streets, their heads turning slowly as though they were searching for something. Mohan's heart raced, and his breath caught in his throat. How was this possible? He shouldn't be able to see anything from his right eye, especially not in the dead of night.

Confusion gripped him, but curiosity drove him forward. His feet moved without thinking, and before he knew it, he was walking toward the figures, the cold wind tugging at his jacket and the rain dripping from his hair. As he got closer, he could see them more clearly—there were three of them, dressed in ragged clothes, their faces pale and expressionless. They moved like shadows, slipping between the dark alleys and side streets as if they belonged to another world.

Mohan's voice broke through the terrible silence. "Hey! Who are you? What are you doing here?" His voice was strong, but beneath it was the tremor of disbelief.

The figures stopped in their tracks, their heads turning in unison to face him. Their eyes widened in fear, and one of them took a step back. They seemed terrified, as if they hadn't expected anyone to see them—especially not someone like Mohan.

"Who… who are you?" one of them stammered, their voice trembling with fear. "Can you see us?" Mohan, still grappling with the impossibility of what was happening, hesitated. He didn't understand how, but he nodded. "Yes… I can see you."

At those words, the figures' fear deepened. They exchanged panicked glances, and without another word, they turned and ran— disappearing into the stormy night like phantoms fleeing from the light. Their movements were swift and unnatural, and within moments, they were gone, swallowed by the shadows and the rain.

Mohan stood frozen, his heart pounding in his chest. He couldn't believe what had just happened. How could he has seen them? His right eye was supposed to be blind, covered by the transplanted eye of his dog. And yet, not only had he seen them, but they had been able to see him—and they had been terrified.

The wind howled around him, pulling at the cloth over his right eye once more. Mohan reached up, touching it gently, his fingers trembling. He had never expected to see through that eye again, and now… now it seemed as though it could see things that weren't meant to be seen.

He turned, hurrying back to the police station, Mohan hurried back through the rain-soaked streets, his mind racing, trying to make sense of what had just happened. His heart still pounded from the strange encounter, but he pushed it deep down, not ready to confront the reality of what he had seen—or what he thought he had seen. The storm continued to rage, the wind whipping around him, and the chill from the night air seeped into his bones.

As he reached the small police station, the dim lights from inside spilled out onto the wet ground. His friend, Ramesh, was pacing anxiously near the entrance, glancing up and down the street, his face tight with worry. The moment he spotted Mohan, relief washed over him, but it was quickly replaced by frustration.

"Mohan! Where the hell were you? I've been waiting for you for over an hour!" Ramesh's voice was sharp, but beneath it, Mohan could hear the genuine concern. "I thought something happened! You should've called me."

Mohan stopped, standing under the awning to catch his breath, the rain dripping off his jacket. His mind was still reeling from what he had just seen, but he forced a casual smile, trying to act as if everything was normal. He didn't want to talk about it—not yet. Maybe not ever

"I'm fine," Mohan said, his voice calmer than he felt. "I just… needed some air"

Ramesh eyed him suspiciously, his brow furrowed as if he knew something wasn't right. But he didn't push it, perhaps sensing that Mohan wasn't ready to talk. "Come on, let's get you home," he said, his tone softening.

Mohan nodded silently, avoiding his friend's gaze. He didn't trust himself to speak. How could he explain what had just happened? How could he tell Ramesh that he had seen people— or things—that shouldn't exist, and that they had been afraid of him? It sounded insane, even to him. So he said nothing.

They climbed into the jeep, the engine rumbling to life as Ramesh pulled out onto the muddy road. The rain hadn't let up, and the windshield wipers struggled to keep up with the downpour. The world outside was a blur of dark shapes and slick streets, the headlights cutting weakly through the storm.

Mohan sat in the passenger seat, staring out the window, but his mind was far from the rain soaked streets of the town. His thoughts kept drifting back to the figures he had seen—their ghostly movements, their pale faces, and the fear in their eyes when he told them he could see them. What were they? Were they real? Or had he finally lost his mind after everything he had been through.

The cloth over his right eye felt heavy, as if the strange encounter had somehow made it more noticeable. He reached up and adjusted it, the feel of the fabric reminding him of the eye beneath—an eye that wasn't truly his. The dog's eye. The eye that had somehow allowed him to see something no one else could. But how was that possible.

The jeep jolted as it hit a pothole, snapping Mohan out of his thoughts. He glanced over at Ramesh, who was focused on the road, his face tense with concentration. Mohan felt a pang of guilt for not telling his friend the truth. Ramesh had been there for him through thick and thin, and yet, Mohan couldn't bring himself to explain what had happened. Not yet.

As they drove through the quiet streets, the storm still raging around them, Mohan's mind kept circling back to the figures he had seen. Their fear, their strange movements, their words—"Can you see us?"—played over and over in his head. Why had they asked that? Why had they been so terrified of him.

"Mohan, you okay?" Ramesh's voice broke through his thoughts, pulling him back to the present. "Yeah," Mohan lied, his voice barely above a whisper. "I'm just tired.

Ramesh glanced at him but didn't press. The rest of the ride was silent, save for the sound of rain hammering the roof and the wipers slashing across the glass. But inside Mohan's mind, the storm was still raging.

As they neared Mohan's house, Ramesh slowed the jeep, the headlights illuminating the narrow lane that led to the front door. The familiar sight of home should have brought some comfort, but instead, it only deepened the unsettling feeling in Mohan's gut. What had he seen tonight? And what did it mean?

The jeep came to a stop, and Ramesh turned to Mohan, his eyes full of concern. "You sure you're okay? You've been quiet all night" Mohan forced a weak smile. "Yeah… just need some sleep"

Ramesh nodded, though he clearly wasn't convinced. "Alright, get some rest. We'll talk tomorrow"

Mohan stepped out of the jeep and into the rain, feeling the cold wind hit his face as he walked toward his door. He paused for a moment, glancing back at Ramesh, who gave him a final worried look before driving away, the taillights disappearing into the storm.

Mohan stood in the rain for a moment longer, staring into the darkness, the uneasy feeling from earlier creeping back into his chest. He couldn't shake the memory of those strange figures, the way they moved, the fear in their eyes. And most of all, he couldn't shake the feeling that something was terribly wrong— that tonight was only the beginning of something far more terrifying than he could imagine. With a deep breath, Mohan turned and entered his home, the storm still raging outside as the mystery of the night haunted his every thought.

CHAPTER 5

The following day, Mohan woke up with a sense of anticipation gnawing at him. His mind had been racing ever since that strange encounter the night before. The strange figures he had seen still haunted his thoughts, and the unsettling question they had asked—"Can you see us?"—echoed in his mind. It was unlike anything he had ever experienced, and he couldn't let it go. He needed answers.

Mohan spent the day in a quiet, restless state. Every time he closed his left eye and focused on his right, the world seemed slightly different— sharper, but not in the usual way. It was as if the eye gave him a view of something beyond what was normal, as if it could see into a realm hidden from most people. He didn't know whether he was excited or terrified by that realization, but one thing was certain: he had to find out more.

But how could he explain this to anyone? His family, his friends—they wouldn't understand. They would think he was losing his mind. Even Ramesh, his closest friend, might dismiss it as stress or the trauma of his accident. No, this was something Mohan had to face alone.

That evening, as the sky began to darken, he made a plan. He told his family he had some urgent work at the station and would be spending the night there. His mother, Kamala Devi, and his wife, Geetha, were concerned, but they didn't question him too much. They could see that he had been restless all day, and they knew Mohan was still struggling with the aftermath of his accident. To them, it seemed like he was just trying to stay busy and distracted.

"I'll be fine," Mohan reassured them with a forced smile. "It's just some paperwork I need to finish up. I'll be back home in the morning." Ramesh, too, had offered to come by the station to keep him company, but Mohan waved it off. "No need," he said casually. "It's just a quiet night shift. I'll be back before you know it."

None of them knew the real reason why Mohan wanted to stay at the station that night. They didn't know that he was waiting for something far more disturbing than paperwork. He needed to see those figures again, to understand what had happened the night before. And deep down, he felt a pull—a strange, unsettling feeling—that those figures would return. The only question was when.

As night fell, Mohan returned to the small, dimly lit station. The air was cool, and the wind had started to pick up again, just as it had the night before. The storm from the previous night had subsided, but the atmosphere remained heavy, as if something was brewing in the darkness. Mohan could feel it— an electric charge in the air that set his nerves on edge.

He settled into the old wooden chair at the station, his left eye scanning the empty room while his right remained hidden beneath the cloth. The hours ticked by slowly, each minute feeling like an eternity. His heart pounded in his chest, not from fear, but from the anticipation of what might come.

Every sound outside seemed amplified—the rustle of leaves in the wind, the distant call of a stray dog, the soft creak of the wooden beams above him. The night was alive in ways it hadn't been before, and Mohan's senses were sharper, more attuned to every detail. He couldn't shake the feeling that he was being watched, that those strange figures were lurking just out of sight, waiting for the right moment to show themselves again.

As midnight approached, Mohan stood up and walked over to the window, staring out into the dark street beyond. The world outside was still and quiet, the dim glow of the streetlights casting long shadows across the wet pavement. But as he closed his left eye, focusing only through the right, the scene shifted. The darkness seemed deeper, the shadows more alive, and for a fleeting moment, he thought he saw something—a movement in the distance, near the alley where he had seen the figures the night before.

His pulse quickened, but he remained calm. This was what he had been waiting for. The answers he sought were out there, somewhere in the dark.

He grabbed his coat and quietly slipped out of the station, his footsteps echoing on the wet ground as he made his way toward the spot where he had first seen the figures. The wind had picked up again, swirling around him in gusts that tugged at his coat and the cloth over his right eye. He walked carefully, his eyes— both of them—scanning the street for any sign of movement.

As he approached the alley, a cold chill ran down his spine. He could feel it—something was watching him, something just beyond his vision. He stopped, his breath coming in slow, deliberate exhales, and then, in the corner of his vision—his right vision—he saw them.

The figures had returned.

They stood at the edge of the alley, barely visible in the shadows, but this time, they were watching him. Their ghostly forms seemed to hover, just as strange and unnatural as the night before. But now, there was something different about them. They weren't moving aimlessly. They were waiting.

Mohan's heart raced, but he forced himself to step forward, his voice steady despite the pounding in his chest. "Who are you?" he asked, louder this time, the wind carrying his words into the night. "Why can I see you?"

The figures didn't move, but one of them, taller than the others, slowly turned its head to look directly at Mohan. Its pale face was expressionless, but its eyes—cold, lifeless eyes— stared at him with an intensity that made Mohan's skin crawl.

"You shouldn't be able to," the figure said, its voice a low, strange whisper that seemed to come from everywhere at once. "You don't belong to our world."

Mohan felt a shiver run through him. The air around him grew colder, and he could feel the weight of their gaze pressing down on him. But he didn't back away. He needed answers.

"What do you mean?" he demanded, stepping closer. "What world are you talking about? Why can I see you now?"

The figure's head tilted slightly, as if it were considering his questions. Then, in a voice barely louder than the wind, it answered, "Because you carry the eyes of one who sees beyond the living."

Mohan froze, his breath catching in his throat. The eye -the dog's eye. It was the reason. He could see them because of the transplant, because of the eye that had once belonged to his loyal companion. But how? How could a dog's eye connect him to whatever these beings were?

Before he could ask anything more, the figures began to fade, their forms dissolving into the darkness like mist in the wind.

"Wait!" Mohan called out, but it was too late. They were gone.

He stood there, alone in the middle of the street, the storm still swirling around him, his mind reeling from what he had just learned.

The night was no longer just a time for darkness. It was a gateway—a gateway to something far more dangerous, something far beyond the world he knew. And now, he was a part of it.

As Mohan turned to head back to the station, his footsteps heavy with the weight of the encounter, something stopped him in his tracks. The air around him seemed to freeze, and an unnatural chill spread over his skin. He could feel a presence behind him. Slowly, cautiously, he turned around.

Standing there in the dim light, barely a few feet away, was a figure. But this one was different from the shadowy ones he had seen before. This figure was clear, its outline sharp against the night sky. It was a man—or at least, it had once been a man. Its pale, translucent skin shimmered slightly in the moonlight, and its hollow eyes stared straight at Mohan.

Mohan's heart pounded. He wanted to move, but his legs wouldn't obey. The figure floated just above the ground, its tattered clothing swaying in the cold wind. Its lips parted, and from its mouth came a low, echoing voice.

"You can see me, can't you?"

Mohan swallowed hard, trying to steady his voice. "W-who are you?"

The ghost's eyes narrowed, as if amused by the question. "It doesn't matter who I am. What matters is that you can see me. And that is… unexpected."

Mohan took a shaky step back, his mind racing. "Why can I see you? What is happening to me?"

The ghost floated a little closer, its voice lowering to a whisper. "Because, Mohan, you have the eyes of a dog. And dogs—" the ghost paused, its cold, lifeless gaze piercing through him, "—can see what humans cannot."

Mohan's heart skipped a beat. "The dog's eye?"

The ghost nodded slowly. "Yes. Dogs can see everything—the living, the dead, the things that hide between worlds. And now, so can you."

Mohan's throat tightened. He could barely get the words out. "This... this isn't possible. I'm human."

The ghost's expression remained unchanged, as if it had seen countless reactions like Mohan's before. "Human, yes. But with a dog's eye, you now walk in both worlds. You see us, the forgotten, the restless. The dead who have not moved on."

Mohan's mind reeled. He felt the blood drain from his face as he processed what he had just heard. "So, I'm seeing ghosts because of the eye?"

The ghost tilted its head, studying him. "Yes. And not just ghosts. There are things far worse than us that dwell in the shadows. And now that you can see, they will see you, too."

Mohan staggered back a step, the weight of those words sinking in. "What do you mean? What kind of things?"

The ghost's voice grew darker, more sinister. "Things that were never human, things that lurk in the dark corners of your world. You are a beacon now, Mohan. You've opened a door that should have remained shut."

Mohan's hands trembled as he reached for the cloth that covered his right eye. His pulse thundered in his ears. "I didn't ask for this."

The ghost let out a soft, hollow laugh. "No one ever does. But now it's too late. The eye sees what it sees. And there is no going back."

Mohan felt his knees weaken as the reality of the situation closed in around him. "What... what do I do?"

The ghost's form began to fade, its voice echoing as it drifted away. "Be careful, Mohan. The world is darker than you think."

"I don't want this. I never asked for these unnatural things." Mohan touched the cloth over his right eye, his expression grim. "I'll find a way to get rid of this dog's eye. I don't want to see ghosts or any of these... things. I just want my normal life back."

The ghost appeared again and hovering in the shadows looked at him with a strange, terrible calmness. "Are you sure, Mohan? Removing the eye won't bring back the life you had before. You've already been touched by the unknown. But this eye... it could be your greatest asset."

Mohan frowned, confused. "How could seeing ghosts ever help me?"

The ghost's voice lowered, becoming almost persuasive. "You can do things no other human can. You can see what others can't, solve what others fail to. Imagine, Mohan—you want to be a great police officer, don't you? With this eye, you can find criminals no one else can catch. I can help you."

Mohan's heart pounded in his chest. The ghost's words tempted him, playing on his deepest desires. "You think... this eye could help me get my job back? To become a better officer?"

The ghost nodded slowly. "Yes. You were demoted because they thought you were no longer fit for duty. But imagine if you started solving the unsolvable cases. Bringing justice where others fail. They'll see your worth again. You'll rise through the ranks faster than ever before. And I will be there, guiding you."

Mohan's eyes widened, his mind racing. It sounded too good to be true. But then he hesitated. "What's the catch? What do you want from me?"

The ghost's voice softened, almost friendly. "I ask for only one thing—keep this between us. No one must know about the dog's eye. You must never speak of it, not to your family, not to your friend. In the daylight, you will see the world as any human would, but at night... you will see what others can't. And with my help, you'll become a successful officer again."

Mohan stared at the ghost, doubt creeping into his mind. "But... what about other ghosts? The unnatural things? What if they come after me?"

The ghost gave a faint, reassuring smile. "They will not harm you as long as I'm with you. You and I—we will work together. I'll help you find the criminals, and in return, you give me companionship. We have a deal, Mohan."

Mohan thought deeply, torn between the fear of the unknown and the burning desire to regain his career and respect. He could picture himself in uniform again, standing tall as an officer, solving the toughest cases. The ghost's offer was tempting, too tempting.

Finally, he looked the ghost in the eye and nodded. "Alright. I'll keep the eye. But remember, this is about justice. I want to catch criminals and help people. If you can help me do that... I'm in."

The ghost's pale face seemed to brighten, its form becoming more solid for a brief moment. "Good. You've made the right choice, Mohan. Together, we will make sure justice is served. And no one will ever know the secret behind your success."

Mohan felt a shiver run down his spine as the ghost's words sank in. He had made a deal with something beyond his understanding, but deep inside, he felt the hope rekindle—the hope that maybe, just maybe, he could get his life back.

As the wind howled and the night deepened, the ghost whispered, "From tonight onward, you and I are partners. And no one will be able to stop us."

CHAPTER 6

The following morning, Mohan stood in front of the mirror, gazing at his reflection with a mixture of disbelief and cautious excitement. He could see clearly from both eyes now—his left and his right. The cloth that had covered his right eye lay discarded on the table. He blinked a few times, testing it, confirming what he already knew: he could see the world again.

Gathering his courage, Mohan stepped out of his room and called for his family. His mother, Kamala Devi, rushed in first, followed by his wife, Geetha, and his cousin, the constable. His friend Ramesh followed closely behind, all of them eager to hear what Mohan had to say.

"I can see again from my right eye ," Mohan announced, a hint of awe still lingering in his voice.

His family gasped. Kamala Devi clutched her chest, her eyes welling with tears of joy. "What did you say, Mohan?"

Mohan smiled, his voice steady. "I can see the world from both eyes. I... I don't know how, but I've recovered."

Geetha's face lit up, and she rushed to embrace him. "This is a miracle, Mohan! A blessing from the gods!"

Even Ramesh, who had always been the rational one, seemed speechless. "Mohan, this is... unbelievable. The doctors said there was no chance you'd regain sight in that eye!"

Mohan nodded, keeping his expression neutral. "I know. I didn't believe it at first either, but I can see now. Everything is clear."

His cousin grinned from ear to ear. "Well, this calls for a celebration! You'll pass the medical test easily now. You'll get your job back in no time!"

Mohan nodded, but deep down, he knew the truth. The "miracle" was not something he could share, not even with those closest to him. He had promised the ghost, and he would keep that promise. The truth of the dog's eye was something he would carry alone.

Later that day, Mohan went to the medical board for his fitness test. The doctors were astonished at his recovery. They ran their examinations, checked his vision, and after a long pause, declared him fit for duty. "This is extraordinary," one of the doctors remarked. "Your recovery is nothing short of miraculous."

Mohan smiled politely, nodding along. "Yes, doctor. It feels like a second chance."

As the news of his recovery spread, his family and friends celebrated. Mohan was reinstated in his police officer position, and as he walked back into the station in uniform, there was a sense of pride and triumph within him.

But that night, as the celebration quieted and the house fell into silence, Mohan felt the pull of something else—the ghost. He waited until everyone was asleep, then made his way through the dark streets to the spot where he had first encountered the apparition. The air was thick with anticipation as he stood there, the cool breeze brushing against his face. Suddenly, the ghost appeared, its translucent figure floating just in front of him.

Mohan took a deep breath and spoke softly, "I came to thank you. If it weren't for you... I wouldn't have my life back. My career, my sight —it's all because of you."

The ghost's hollow eyes gleamed as it replied, "You've done well, Mohan. But this is just the beginning."

Mohan's brow furrowed. "What do you mean?"

The ghost's voice was low, almost whispering, as it drew closer. "You've regained your position. But now... now you have the power to become more successful than any other officer in this city. With my help, you will catch the criminals no one else can. You will be feared by those who walk in the shadows. You will be invincible."

Mohan felt a surge of excitement, his pulse quickening at the thought. "You really believe I can do all that?"

The ghost let out a soft, chilling laugh. "You are not like other men anymore, Mohan. You see things they cannot even fathom. You are special. And together, we will make sure that no criminal goes unpunished."

Mohan smiled, his gratitude overflowing. "Thank you... thank you for everything."

The ghost's expression remained cold but pleased. "Remember, Mohan—our bond must remain a secret. No one can know about the eye or about me. You must continue as if nothing has changed, but in the night... we will work together. We will hunt those who believe they are untouchable."

Mohan nodded, his mind racing with the possibilities. "I understand. I won't tell anyone."

The ghost floated back slightly, its form beginning to fade. "Good. Then be ready. Your journey has only just begun."

As the ghost disappeared into the night, Mohan stood there, his heart pounding in his chest. He had made a deal with something beyond his comprehension, and there was no turning back now. But the thought of becoming a legendary officer, of making a real difference, filled him with a dangerous sense of hope.

Mohan walked back toward his home, the cool night air brushing against his face, and smiled to himself. He was ready to embrace whatever the future had in store.

As he whispered into the night, "This is just the beginning," a soft echo of the ghost's voice seemed to linger in the wind, "Indeed, it is."

The first week after Mohan returned to his duties was quiet, almost unnervingly so. He felt the strange calm in the city like the silence before a storm. His colleagues welcomed him back with smiles and pats on the back, but Mohan could sense something dark looming over the horizon. And sure enough, it wasn't long before the storm hit.

A notorious criminal gang had made its way into the city. They were ruthless—engaging in theft, kidnapping, and trafficking. Their reign of terror spread quickly, and within days, fear gripped the city. News of their heinous activities reached every corner, and the pressure mounted on the police to act.

One afternoon, an emergency meeting was called at the police station. All the top officers were present, gathered around the table in the dimly lit conference room. Their faces were grim, weighed down by the gravity of the situation.

The chief of police cleared his throat, standing at the head of the table. "We've got a serious problem on our hands, and the people are looking to us for answers. This gang has already made a name for itself in other cities, and they've brought their chaos here now. We can't afford to let this escalate any further."

One of the senior officers spoke up, his voice laced with frustration. "But this isn't like any ordinary gang. They're smart, they have connections, and they're always one step ahead. We've tried everything—surveillance, informants, but they're notorious."

Mohan, who had been listening quietly from the back of the room, stepped forward. "Sir, if I may..."

All eyes turned toward him, and the room went silent. The chief raised an eyebrow. "Yes, Mohan?"

Mohan took a deep breath, feeling the presence of the ghost at the edge of his thoughts, urging him on. "I'd like to take the lead in catching this gang."

There were murmurs around the room, some sceptical, some surprised. One of the senior officers leaned forward, frowning. "Mohan, this isn't just any operation. These men are dangerous, and we can't afford mistakes. You've only just returned. Perhaps you should sit this one out."

Mohan stood his ground, his voice steady. "I understand the risk, sir. But I'm ready. I know this city like the back of my hand, and I've dealt with criminals before. Give me a team, and I'll bring them in."

The chief looked at Mohan for a long moment, then exchanged glances with the other officers. "Mohan, this is not just about being brave. These men... they're brutal, and they're well protected. It's a dangerous assignment, and we need someone who's at the peak of their physical and mental ability."

Mohan clenched his jaw. He could feel the doubts in the room, but he also felt the cold confidence of the ghost lingering near him, whispering silent encouragement. "Sir, I won't let you down. I can do this. With all due respect, I'm the best person for this job."

Another officer scoffed. "Mohan, we're not questioning your will, but the odds are stacked against you. You've only been back a week, and you're still recovering."

Mohan's eyes darkened, his determination steeling his voice. "Trust me, just give me this chance."

There was a long pause. The room was tense. Finally, the chief sighed and nodded. "Fine. It's your responsibility. But don't forget, Mohan— there's no room for failure. The city is counting on us."

Mohan nodded sharply. "I won't fail."

That night, as the city slept, Mohan stood alone on a rooftop, his gaze sweeping over the city's sprawling streets below. The ghost appeared beside him, its ethereal form hovering in the moonlight.

"You've taken on a great burden, Mohan," the ghost whispered, its voice echoing in the silence. "Are you ready for what's to come?"

Mohan didn't hesitate. "With your help, I can catch them. Tell me where they are."

The ghost's eyes gleamed. "They are hiding in places you cannot see with human eyes. But with the dog's eye, you will find them. They operate under the cover of night, where no human dares tread. But you... you are not just a man anymore."

Mohan felt a shiver run down his spine. "Show me the way."

Over the next few days, Mohan worked tirelessly, tracking the gang's movements with the ghost's guidance. While other officers hit dead ends, Mohan seemed to know exactly where to look. He moved through the shadows of the city, using his enhanced vision to spot hidden clues, overhear secret conversations, and track the criminals' movements.

The ghost whispered names, locations, and plans into his ear. Mohan was relentless, swooping down on the gang members like a predator, arresting them one by one. His colleagues watched in awe as Mohan seemed to pull off the impossible. He dismantled the gang's operations with precision and speed, catching their leader in a daring late-night raid that no one else could have pulled off.

A week later, Mohan stood before the entire police force, dressed in his uniform, his badge gleaming in the light. The chief of police stepped forward, clapping him on the shoulder.

"Mohan Kumar," he said proudly, "you have not only proven yourself but have gone beyond what any of us expected. Your bravery and sharp instincts have brought this gang to justice. For that, you have the department's deepest gratitude."

The room erupted in applause. Mohan's family stood at the back, beaming with pride. His colleagues congratulated him, but only Mohan knew the truth of what had happened—the secret he had sworn to keep.

As the chief handed Mohan his new promotion papers, announcing his rise to a higher post, the ghost's voice echoed softly in Mohan's mind. "This is only the beginning. We will rise further still. Together, we will make this city ours."

Mohan smiled, accepting the promotion. But deep inside, he knew that his journey was far from over. With the ghost by his side, the line between justice and something darker had begun to blur.

As the applause filled the room, Mohan whispered under his breath, "Thank you... for everything."

And somewhere in the shadows, the ghost smiled back, waiting for their next move.

CHAPTER 7

As time passed, Mohan's reputation as a brilliant and unstoppable police officer grew rapidly throughout the city. His ability to solve even the most perplexing and dangerous cases left his colleagues in awe. What they didn't know, however, was that behind his newfound success stood the ghost—his silent partner, his unseen ally.

Every night, Mohan and the ghost worked together, unearthing clues that no other detective could find. The ghost's knowledge of the supernatural world gave Mohan an edge that made him unstoppable.

One late evening, Mohan sat alone in his small office at the police station, staring at the latest case file. A series of brutal murders had rocked the city, and the killer had left behind no evidence—no fingerprints, no witnesses. The entire department was baffled.

Just then, the ghost appeared, hovering near the window, its translucent form barely visible in the dim light.

"Mohan," the ghost whispered, its voice soft but urgent, "this is no ordinary killer."

Mohan looked up, nodding. "I figured as much. There's something strange about this case... something that doesn't feel right."

The ghost floated closer, its eyes glowing faintly. "The killer moves through shadows, slipping between this world and the next. No human can catch him... but we can."

Mohan leaned back in his chair, a determined look in his eyes. "Tell me what I need to do."

The ghost's voice took on a chilling tone. "You must go where no one else dares to go. To the abandoned building on the outskirts of the city. That's where he hides, where he draws his power. But be warned—what you find there may not be human."

Mohan didn't hesitate. "I'm ready."

Later that night, Mohan arrived at the decrepit building, the moon casting a strange glow over the crumbling structure. As he approached, the ghost materialized beside him, guiding him through the maze of shadows.

"This place is cursed," the ghost murmured. "Be careful."

Mohan's heart pounded as he stepped inside, his flashlight barely piercing the thick darkness. Suddenly, a cold wind swept through the room, and he saw movement in the corner of his eye ,something inhuman lurking in the shadows.

Without hesitation, Mohan whispered, "Show yourself."

A figure emerged from the darkness, its face twisted and unnatural. The killer had been hiding, using dark powers to avoid detection. But with the ghost's help, Mohan saw through the veil of fear that had kept others away. The killer, sensing Mohan's connection to the supernatural, tried to flee, but

Mohan's reflexes were too quick. He apprehended the figure in a swift, calculated move.

Back at the station, the department was in awe. "How did you find him, Mohan?" one of his colleagues asked, shaking his head in disbelief.

Mohan simply smiled and shrugged. "I had a feeling," he replied, knowing the ghost's assistance had been crucial.

As the months passed, more challenging cases came Mohan's way—missing persons, unsolved murders, and criminals who seemed to vanish without a trace. Each time, Mohan leaned on the ghost for guidance, and together, they cracked every case.

One evening, after another successful operation, Mohan sat on the rooftop of the station, staring out at the city skyline. The ghost appeared next to him, its form glowing softly in the moonlight.

"We make quite the team," Mohan said, a satisfied smile on his face.

The ghost nodded. "Yes, we do. But remember, Mohan, the more you rely on me, the further you step into my world."

Mohan was silent for a moment, staring at the horizon. He knew the ghost was right. Their bond was growing stronger with every case they solved, and with it, the line between the natural and supernatural was blurring.

"I don't regret it," Mohan finally said. "We've done a lot of good together. And I'm willing to keep going, as long as it means making this city safer."

The ghost smiled faintly, its eyes glowing with approval. "Then we shall continue. There is much more work to be done."

Mohan nodded, feeling a deep sense of loyalty to the ghost that had helped him so much. "Let's make this city ours."

The next day, Mohan's name was on every headline in the city. The press hailed him as the best police officer the city had ever seen. Promotions and accolades poured in, and his colleagues spoke of him with respect and admiration. But Mohan knew the truth—that none of it would have been possible without the ghost's help.

Late at night, Mohan would retreat to the darkness, where he and the ghost would meet to discuss their next move. Their partnership had become a force of justice, one that no criminal could evade. And as their friendship deepened, Mohan found himself trusting the ghost more and more, even as the dangers of their connection grew.

But for now, he was content. Together, they had solved the unsolvable, and Mohan had become the hero of the city.

In one of their many late-night conversations, Mohan leaned against the wall, a smile playing on his lips. "You know, I never imagined I'd be here—so close to solving these big cases."

The ghost hovered near, its voice soft and knowing. "And you have just begun. There are still greater challenges ahead, Mohan. You have seen what others cannot. You have a gift now, a gift that can change everything."

Mohan nodded thoughtfully, his eyes reflecting the quiet ambition that burned within him. "With you by my side, there's no case we can't solve."

The ghost's smile widened. "Exactly ,And soon, the city will see that no one can hide from us— not in this world, nor the next."

As the days turned into months, Mohan's success story spread across the city like wildfire. Every corner of the police department buzzed with stories of his brilliance, his knack for solving the toughest cases, and his unwavering dedication. Criminals feared him, citizens admired him, and his colleagues respected him. His name became synonymous with justice.

One fine day, Mohan received the news he had only dared to dream of: he was being promoted to the position of Chief Police Officer, the highest rank in the city. His childhood dream had come true, a dream he thought had been shattered by the accident. But now, thanks to the ghost's help, it was his reality.

That evening, Mohan sat in his new office—a spacious room overlooking the bustling city. The desk was adorned with a nameplate that read 'Chief Mohan Kumar' in bold letters. He ran his fingers over it, a proud smile on his face. His heart swelled with a mixture of pride and gratitude, knowing deep down that none of this would have been possible without the ghost's guidance.

As if on cue, the ghost appeared in the corner of the room, its translucent figure glowing faintly in the dim light.

"You've done well, Mohan," the ghost said, its voice filled with satisfaction. "You've achieved what you once thought was impossible."

Mohan turned to the ghost, his eyes reflecting his happiness. "I couldn't have done it without you," he said sincerely. "Everything—this position, my reputation, my success—it's all because of you."

The ghost hovered closer, its smile widening. "I promised you I'd help you, and I have. But remember, this is only the beginning. As long as we work together, there's no limit to what you can achieve."

Mohan nodded, fully believing in the ghost's words. "I trust you completely. Together, we've made this city a safer place. And we'll continue to do so."

His success had also brought immense joy to his family. His mother, Kamala Devi, beamed with pride whenever she spoke of her son's achievements. His wife, Geetha, was overjoyed, her eyes sparkling with happiness as she watched Mohan's dreams come true. Even his close friend, Ramesh, couldn't stop praising him.

One evening, as they all sat around the dinner table, Geetha said, "Mohan, you've come such a long way. I remember the days when you used to talk about becoming a chief police officer. Now, look at you!"

Mohan smiled, a deep sense of fulfilment washing over him. "It feels like a dream," he said softly. "There were times I thought I'd lost everything—my career, my vision. But here I am, with everything I ever wanted."

Ramesh, sitting across from him, raised his glass in a toast. "To Mohan, the best Chief Police Officer this city has ever had!" Everyone cheered, the room filled with laughter and joy.

Yet, deep inside, Mohan knew the truth. His success, his rise to power, wasn't just the result of his hard work—it was the ghost that had led him here. Every major decision he had made, every case he had solved, had been under the ghost's guidance. And for that, he was eternally grateful.

Late that night, Mohan stood on the balcony of his home, looking out at the city he now protected. The ghost appeared beside him, as it always did in moments of quiet reflection.

"I owe you everything," Mohan said, his voice sincere. "Without you, I'd be nothing."

The ghost's eyes gleamed, its tone filled with pride. "You've earned your success, Mohan. You had the will, the drive. I only showed you the way. Together, we've created a legacy."

Mohan smiled, feeling a deep sense of contentment. "I won't let you down. We'll keep working together, making this city the safest place it's ever been."

The ghost nodded. "I know you won't. Our partnership is stronger than ever."

As the days went by, Mohan continued to excel in his role as Chief Police Officer. He implemented new policies, cracked down on crime, and led his team with the same determination that had brought him this far. The city thrived under his leadership, and Mohan's name became legendary.

But through it all, Mohan never forgot the ghost's role in his success. He kept the secret of the dog's eye hidden, just as he had promised. And every night, when the world was asleep, he would meet with the ghost, discussing their next steps, planning how to keep the city safe.

One night, as they stood on the balcony again, the ghost said, "Mohan, you've become everything you once dreamed of. But don't forget—there's always more to achieve."

Mohan smiled, the fire of ambition still burning in his chest. "I'm ready for whatever comes next," he said confidently. "As long as we're together, nothing can stop us."

The ghost smiled back, its form shimmering in the moonlight. "Exactly. This city is ours, and we will protect it—no matter what."

And so, Mohan's reign as the Chief Police Officer continued, marked by success, honour, and the unbreakable bond he shared with the ghost. Together, they were a force to be reckoned with —one that the city would never forget.

CHAPTER 8

One night, the city was shrouded in an unsettling calm, the kind of quiet that usually comes before a storm. The faint hum of streetlights and the occasional rumble of cars were the only sounds piercing the silence. Suddenly, the calm was broken by the loud screech of tires, followed by the unmistakable sound of a crash. A car had collided with a lamp post at the intersection of two deserted streets, and within minutes, the police were on the scene.

Mohan, now the Chief Police Officer, arrived shortly after. His eyes scanned the area, quickly taking in the details—the crushed front end of the car, the skid marks on the road, the shattered glass strewn across the pavement. A few witnesses stood nearby, but no one seemed to have seen much. It looked like a straightforward accident, the result of speeding on a rainy night.

As Mohan crouched beside the wrecked car, his flashlight flickering over the broken windshield, his instincts told him there was nothing suspicious here. He examined the scene carefully, ensuring no detail was missed. "It looks like a simple accident," he muttered under his breath, making notes in his mind.

Just as he was about to instruct his team to wrap up, the ghost appeared beside him, its presence sending a cold chill through the air. Mohan immediately stood up straight, his hand tightening around his flashlight. The ghost's expression was serious, its voice low and foreboding.

"This is not what it seems, Mohan," the ghost said, hovering close to the wreckage. "It may look like an accident, but there's more to it."

Mohan frowned, his eyes narrowing as he looked at the ghost. "What do you mean? Everything here points to a simple car crash— no signs of foul play, no strange behaviour, just a driver losing control."

The ghost shook its head, its voice carrying a note of warning. "That's exactly what they want you to think. Some accidents are more than they appear—this one is no mere mishap. This is a carefully planned murder, disguised to fool everyone. Look closer, Mohan. Think about what's missing, not just what's here."

Mohan took a deep breath, his gaze shifting from the ghost to the wrecked car. He trusted the ghost's judgment—after all, it had helped him countless times before. He began to re-examine the scene, this time with a sharper focus. He walked around the car, paying attention to every detail.

"But there's no sign of tampering," Mohan said, though now his voice held a note of uncertainty. "No broken brakes, no sabotage…"

The ghost floated closer to him, its voice firm. "Not all murders leave obvious clues, Mohan. The best ones are invisible to the untrained eye. Look at the position of the car, the timing of the crash. Why was there no attempt to brake before impact? Why was the victim alone in a place where he never usually drives?"

Mohan's mind raced as he absorbed the ghost's words. The rain had been light earlier in the evening, not enough to cause someone to lose control like this. He thought back to the victim— a businessman, known to be cautious. Why would he be speeding on such a night?

The ghost's voice grew even quieter, almost a whisper. "There's more at play here. You need to dig deeper. Find out who stood to gain from this man's death. People don't kill without reason, but they're clever. They know how to make murder look like an accident."

Mohan nodded, his conviction growing. "You're right," he said softly. "There's something off about all of this." He straightened, his mind now whirring with possibilities. "I'll start by looking into the victim's connections. Someone had a reason to kill him, and I'll find out who."

The ghost hovered close, its translucent form flickering slightly. "Good. But be careful, Mohan. Not everyone will be happy if you uncover the truth. And remember—some of the most dangerous criminals are the ones who hide in plain sight, pretending to be innocent."

The next day, Mohan dove into the investigation with renewed energy. His team continued treating it as an accident, but Mohan's instincts, sharpened by the ghost's words, led him in a different direction. He began digging into the victim's personal life—his business dealings, his family connections, his rivals. The more he uncovered, the more he realized how many people had a motive for wanting the businessman dead.

Late that evening, Mohan met with Ramesh in his office. His friend raised an eyebrow as he saw the stack of papers on Mohan's desk. "I thought you said this was just an accident?"

Mohan shook his head, his face grim. "That's what I thought at first. But now, I'm not so sure. There's something else going on here. I think this was a planned murder, disguised to look like a crash."

Ramesh's eyes widened. "Are you serious? What makes you think that?"

Mohan glanced toward the window, the memory of the ghost's words still fresh in his mind. "Let's just say… I've got a gut feeling. There's more to this story than we realize."

Ramesh leaned forward, intrigued. "So, what's your next move?"

Mohan looked back at him, determination shining in his eyes. "I'm going to find out who's behind this. And when I do, they'll regret ever trying to pull something like this under my watch.''

As night fell once again, Mohan knew he had only scratched the surface of the mystery. But with the ghost by his side, he was confident that the truth would come out—and that justice, as always, would prevail.

One evening, after solving the case and bringing the criminals to justice, Mohan was overwhelmed with pride and satisfaction. The city's chief of police had once again proven his capability, and he knew that without the ghost's help, this complex investigation might have taken a darker turn. Mohan wanted to share his happiness with the one who had stood by him from the shadows—the ghost.

As he sat alone in his dimly lit office, waiting for the ghost to appear, he felt a strange sense of anticipation. Tonight, he wanted to express his gratitude, to acknowledge how much the ghost had helped him succeed. He had learned to rely on its guidance, and in many ways, the ghost had become his secret ally.

Soon enough, the ghost materialized before him, but something felt different. Its presence was not the same as before—there was heaviness in the air, and the usually calm demeanour of the ghost seemed tense.

"Good evening, my friend," Mohan began, trying to keep the tone light, though he noticed the ghost's silent stare. "I just wanted to thank you. We've done something incredible together, solving this case. The city is safer because of us."

The ghost hovered for a moment, its ethereal form wavering slightly in the shadows. Then it spoke, its voice colder than usual. "Yes, Mohan. We've done well. But I have something I need to ask you."

Mohan frowned, feeling the shift in tone. "Of course. Ask me anything."

The ghost's eyes, once calm, seemed to flicker with an intensity Mohan hadn't seen before. "You've achieved so much in your career, Mohan. You've become the chief of police, a respected leader. But tell me—what is the most important thing in your life now?"

Mohan was taken aback. The question felt strange, almost like a test. He paused, thinking carefully before he answered. "Well… it's my duty, of course. As the chief, I've sworn to uphold justice. To protect the innocent and ensure criminals are punished for their wrongdoings."

The ghost remained silent, its form shifting slightly as though deep in thought. Then, in a more serious tone, it asked again. "And what about your family, Mohan? Where do they stand in comparison to your duty? Is justice more important than your family?"

Mohan's heart skipped a beat. He wasn't expecting such a question. "My family? What kind of question is that?" he asked, trying to dismiss the unease growing in his chest. "Why are you asking me this? Of course, my family is important to me. But… justice—justice is my purpose." The ghost did not relent. "I want to know, Mohan. Which is more important to you? Your family or justice?"

Mohan shifted uncomfortably in his chair, feeling the weight of the ghost's piercing gaze. "Why are you pressing me like this? Both are important, but I've sworn an oath to protect the city. Justice is at the core of my life, and it's something I've worked for my entire career."

The ghost moved closer, its voice dropping to a whisper. "I need a clear answer. If you were ever faced with a choice— between protecting your family and delivering justice—what would you choose? Your wife, your mother, or your duty?"

Mohan felt his throat tighten. This wasn't just an ordinary question—it was a challenge, a moral dilemma. He tried to think rationally, but the ghost's insistence unnerved him. He looked away, confused, unsure of what to say.

"You're making me uncomfortable," Mohan admitted, his voice shaky. "Why would you ask me something like that? What are you trying to prove?"

The ghost's voice was firm, echoing through the room. "Because one day, Mohan, you may face this choice. And when that time comes, I want to know what kind of man you truly are. So, tell me. Will you choose justice, or will you choose your family?"

Mohan sat in silence, his mind racing. After a long pause, he finally spoke, his voice steady but filled with uncertainty.

"I… I've dedicated my life to upholding justice. No matter how painful the choice, I will always put justice first. It's what makes me who I am. It's my duty."

The ghost watched him closely, its expression unreadable. Then, slowly, it began to smile—a cold, satisfied smile.

"Good, Mohan. You've given me the answer I wanted to hear," the ghost said, its voice soft but filled with a strange satisfaction. "You are a man of justice. That is why I have chosen to help you."

Mohan, still confused by the ghost's line of questioning, felt a knot form in his stomach. "I don't understand. Why is this so important to you? Why ask me such things?"

The ghost's smile remained. "Because, Mohan, there are forces in this world—both seen and unseen—that test the limits of your loyalty, your resolve. You may think you've seen everything, but trust me, there's more to come. And when that time comes, I'll be by your side, guiding you. Just remember—justice is never easy, and it always demands sacrifice."

Mohan felt a chill run down his spine. The ghost's words lingered in his mind, and even as the spirit faded into the shadows, he couldn't shake the feeling that something far deeper was at play.

"Justice is everything," Mohan whispered to himself, trying to convince his own heart. But the doubt lingered, creeping into his thoughts like a shadow he couldn't escape. What had the ghost truly meant?

CHAPTER 9

It was a quiet evening when Mohan sat in his living room, laughing and reminiscing with his cousin. They were both enjoying the warmth of the house as the wind howled softly outside. Mohan was sharing his stories of rising through the ranks in the police force, recounting his early struggles and triumphs. His cousin listened intently, nodding and occasionally laughing at Mohan's lighter anecdotes.

"You've come a long way, Mohan," his cousin remarked, leaning back in his chair. "From a small clerical role to becoming the chief of police in this city. It's quite impressive."

Mohan smiled. "It hasn't been easy, but I've had good support. You, Ramesh, and my family… I'm grateful for everything."

Just as the conversation reached its most relaxed point, the temperature in the room seemed to drop. A familiar chill filled the air, and Mohan's expression changed as he noticed the ghost materialize in the corner of the room, its form visible only to him. He stiffened, knowing this wasn't a casual visit.

The ghost's eyes flickered toward his cousin. Mohan quickly realized the ghost wanted to speak in private.

"Brother," Mohan said, trying to maintain his composure, "I just remembered something from the station I need to handle. Could you head out for a while? We'll catch up later."

His cousin nodded, not suspecting anything. "Of course. I'll see you later then."

As soon as the door shut behind his cousin, the ghost moved forward, its face stern and serious. Mohan stood up, sensing something was wrong.

"What is it? You seem different tonight," Mohan asked cautiously.

The ghost's voice was cold and deliberate. "You were sitting with the man who tried to kill you, Mohan."

Mohan felt his heart skip a beat. "What?" he whispered in disbelief, staring at the ghost. "You can't be serious. My cousin? He's family. Why would he want to harm me?"

The ghost's gaze never wavered. "Your cousin orchestrated your accident. The one that nearly killed you in the jungle. Do you remember? You lost your eye, your loyal dog… That was no mere accident, Mohan. It was a calculated move, and your cousin was behind it."

Mohan's mouth went dry. "No, this can't be true. He's family. He wouldn't…" His voice trailed off, conflicted and confused.

The ghost remained firm. "Remember the holiday tour? You, your family, Ramesh, and your cousin went to the jungle for some peace. But you had to leave early because of an emergency call from work. Before you left, your cousin did something to your jeep, ensuring the accident would happen."

Mohan shook his head, still in shock. "I don't believe it. He was with us the whole time. Why would he do that? He's been supportive; he's helped me through everything..."

The ghost leaned closer, its voice lowering but growing more intense. "Think back, Mohan. Why your jeep met accident with car in the jungle, where no help could reach you for hours? Luckily you survive but lose your eye and your dog. Your cousin knew about your schedule, knew you would be alone in that jeep. He tampered with it, and I can give you the evidence you need."

Mohan felt his hands tremble slightly. His mind raced, trying to process what he was hearing. "But… why? Why would he want to harm me?" His voice wavered, searching for something to cling to.

The ghost's reply was calm yet devastating. "Jealousy, Resentment. Your success has overshadowed him, and he fears losing his place in your life. He saw an opportunity when you went on that tour. You've risen to power, but not everyone is happy about it."

Mohan sat down, gripping the edge of the table. "This is madness…"he muttered, his mind replaying the events of that night over and over. "But… what can I do now?"

The ghost's presence seemed to loom larger, filling the room with a pressing intensity. "Now comes the real test, Mohan. You've always claimed to be a man of justice. So tell me, will you protect your cousin, or will you bring him to justice? The choice is yours, but remember—you've vowed to stand for truth and fairness above all else."

Mohan stared at the ghost, his thoughts swirling. He was speechless, torn between his loyalty to family and his unyielding commitment to justice. "I don't know…" he began, his voice cracking. "How can I turn against him without knowing everything? How can I accuse him based on this?"

The ghost tilted its head, watching him closely. "I told you I could provide the evidence. I will show you what he did, how he tampered with the jeep. You will know the truth. But you must decide if you can handle it."

Mohan's mind was a battlefield of emotions. He had always believed in the rule of law, in justice for all, but this was different. This was his family—his cousin, someone who had been by his side for years.

"What will you do, Mohan?" the ghost's voice echoed, its tone demanding an answer.

Mohan exhaled deeply, his gaze fixed on the floor. "I… I need to see the proof, "he finally said, his voice heavy with sorrow." If this is true, then I have to act. Justice is what I've dedicated my life to. Even if it's painful, I can't turn away from it."

The ghost nodded, its expression softening slightly. "Very well. I'll show you the truth. But be prepared, Mohan. The road ahead will not be easy."

Mohan remained silent, his heart heavy with the burden of the decision that lay before him. For the first time in his life, he felt utterly helpless, caught between duty and blood.

"Justice or family," he whispered to himself, his voice barely audible in the quiet room. "How can I choose?"

The days following Mohan's discovery were some of the hardest he had ever faced. He had asked the ghost for evidence, and the ghost had delivered. The proof was undeniable—his cousin had tampered with the jeep, causing the accident that nearly killed Mohan and took the life of his loyal dog. There was no turning back now.

One evening, Mohan sat alone in his office, staring at the photographs, documents, and recordings that the ghost had brought him. His cousin's betrayal stung deeply. His hand rested on his desk, trembling slightly as he thought about what he had to do next.

The door creaked open, and Ramesh walked in, his face filled with concern. "Mohan, I heard what you're planning. You can't be serious about arresting your own cousin. He's family!"

Mohan looked up, his face a mask of torment. "I have no choice, Ramesh. The evidence is clear. He tried to kill me."

Ramesh shook his head, pacing the room. "But Mohan, this is your blood! How can you send him to prison? We've known him for years. He's always been by your side."

Mohan sighed deeply, the weight of his decision pressing heavily on his chest. "I know, Ramesh. But justice is justice. I can't ignore the truth just because he's family."

At that moment, Geetha, Mohan's wife, entered the room, her eyes filled with tears. "Mohan, please... don't do this. He's your cousin. He's been with us through everything. You can't destroy him like this."

Mohan stood up, his voice soft but firm. "Geetha, if it had been someone else, you wouldn't be asking me to protect them. Justice has to be blind. He betrayed me, betrayed all of us. If I don't act now, I'll be betraying everything I stand for."

Geetha walked toward him, pleading. "Mohan, I'm begging you. Think about your family. Your mother won't survive this heartbreak. You'll tear everything apart!"

Mohan clenched his fists, struggling to hold back his own emotions. "Do you think this is easy for me? Do you think I don't feel the same pain? But if I let him go, what kind of man am I? What kind of police officer? I've sworn to uphold justice, even if it costs me everything."

Just then, Kamala Devi, his mother, appeared at the door. Her eyes were red, swollen from crying. "Mohan, I raised you to be a good man, a man of honour. But… this is your cousin. My nephew. How can you do this? Please, for the sake of our family, reconsider."

Mohan's heart wrenched at the sight of his mother, but he stood resolute. "I wish there was another way. But if I don't act, I'm no better than the criminals I fight. I'm betraying my duty to justice. If I let this go, how can I look anyone in the eye again?"

Kamala wiped her tears, her voice cracking. "But he's family, Mohan. Family comes first."

Mohan shook his head, fighting back his own tears. "No, Justice comes first."

The room was heavy with silence. His wife, his mother, and his best friend all stared at him, their eyes pleading, their hearts shattered. But Mohan couldn't change his mind. He had to do what was right.

The next morning, Mohan made the hardest arrest of his life. His cousin stood before him, confused, angry, and hurt. "Mohan, you're really doing this? After everything we've been through?" his cousin asked, his voice trembling.

Mohan swallowed the lump in his throat. "I have to. I'm sorry."

His cousin was led away in handcuffs, and as Mohan watched, his heart felt heavier than ever. His family's pleas echoed in his mind, but he couldn't waver now. He had chosen justice.

Later that evening, the ghost appeared once again. It floated before Mohan, its face calm and serene.

"You did it, Mohan," the ghost said, its voice filled with approval. "You put justice above all else. Even when your own family begged you to turn a blind eye, you stood firm."

Mohan sat down, his head in his hands. "But it doesn't feel like a victory. I've lost so much. My family… they'll never forgive me."

The ghost floated closer. "In the end, Mohan, you did what few can do. You upheld the law without letting emotion cloud your judgment. That is the mark of a true officer of justice."

Mohan looked up, his eyes filled with pain. "But was it worth it? My mother… my wife… they're devastated."

The ghost nodded. "Sacrifice is part of the path you've chosen. But remember this—justice is not always kind, and it is rarely easy. You've done what many would fear to do. You stood for what was right."

Mohan closed his eyes, exhaling deeply. "I just wish I didn't feel so alone in this."

The ghost placed its hand on Mohan's shoulder. "You are not alone. You have earned my respect, and together, we will continue to bring justice to this city. You are destined for greatness, Mohan, and this is only the beginning."

Mohan nodded slowly, though the ache in his chest remained. "Thank you," he whispered, unsure if he was speaking to the ghost or to himself.

And as the ghost vanished into the shadows, Mohan sat in silence, knowing that while justice had been served, the cost of it weighed heavily on his soul.

CHAPTER 10

It was a calm evening when Mohan sat with Geetha, his wife, and Ramesh, his trusted friend, in their living room. The conversation was light, filled with laughter and old memories. They were talking about their past and the hurdles they had overcome together, especially Mohan's miraculous return to full vision and his rise to the top position in the police force.

As Mohan leaned back in his chair, content, something stirred in the corner of the room. He glanced toward the window and there it was— the ghost, its face unusually stern. It beckoned silently, its hand making an urgent motion. Mohan felt a knot tighten in his stomach. Something was wrong.

"Excuse me for a minute," Mohan said to Geetha and Ramesh, his voice steady despite the tension rising inside him. "I just need to check something outside."

Geetha gave him a curious glance. "At this hour?"

Mohan forced a smile. "It's nothing, I'll be right back." Ramesh raised an eyebrow but said nothing.

Mohan stepped out into the night, closing the door behind him. His face immediately hardened as he turned to the ghost. "What's going on? Why do you look so… disturbed?"

The ghost hovered before him, its once calm demeanour replaced with deep unease. Its voice, when it spoke, was low and troubled. "Mohan… this is serious. Very serious."

Mohan frowned, crossing his arms. "Tell me what it is. What's so urgent?"

The ghost hesitated, its form flickering slightly as if it was battling with itself. "There's something I've been reluctant to tell you, but I can't keep it from you any longer. It's about your accident—the one in the jungle where you lost your dog, your eye… and nearly your life."

Mohan's eyes narrowed. "What about it? You already told me, my cousin was involved, and I dealt with that. He's in jail."

The ghost shook its head, its voice dropping to a near whisper. "There were others involved that night."

Mohan's heart skipped a beat. "Others? Who?"

The ghost's gaze was steady, but its words were laced with hesitation. "Your wife, Geetha… and your friend, Ramesh."

Mohan's face went white. "What? No. No! That's impossible. They would never… How dare you say that?" His voice rose, thick with disbelief and anger. He felt his heart pound in his chest, his mind reeling from the accusation.

The ghost remained calm, though its tone was heavy. "Mohan, I wish I didn't have to tell you this. But it's the truth. I've gathered the evidence —there were things they did to your jeep that night, things that ensured it would fail. Your cousin wasn't the only one who betrayed you."

Mohan shook his head violently. "You're lying! They're my family! My wife and my best friend! They would never… why would they want me dead?"

The ghost sighed deeply, knowing how much the revelation would hurt. "Mohan, there's something going on between them. They've been drawn to each other for some time now. They believed that if you were out of the way, they could be together."

Mohan felt the ground beneath him give way. He staggered backward, his mind clouded with disbelief. "No… no, that's not possible. Geetha loves me. Ramesh is my friend, my brother. This can't be real."

The ghost floated closer, its voice grave. "I'm not saying this lightly, Mohan. They plotted against you because of their secret relationship. I have the proof. I can show you everything— every detail of what they did."

Mohan clenched his fists, his breath shallow and uneven. "I can't… I can't believe this. After everything we've been through. After everything we've faced together. This is some kind of mistake."

The ghost's voice softened, but its words were firm. "It's not a mistake, Mohan. The evidence is clear. I know this is the hardest truth you've ever had to face, but you need to ask yourself: are you a man of justice, or will you let your emotions blind you?"

Mohan's head spun. He thought about the justice he had upheld, the criminals he had taken down, his cousin who now sat in a jail cell. And now, his family—the two people closest to him—were being accused of the same betrayal. His hands trembled, and his voice cracked as he whispered, "Why me? Why would they do this to me?"

The ghost's tone was almost sympathetic.

"They thought they could have a future together without you in the way. But now that you know the truth, you have a decision to make. Will you bring them to justice, or will you let them get away with this crime because they are your family?"

Mohan stood there, torn between rage and despair. He wanted to scream, to confront Geetha and Ramesh right then, but the ghost's words echoed in his mind: justice or family?

He turned to the ghost, his voice barely above a whisper. "How can I do this? How can I face them now?"

The ghost replied softly, but with conviction. "The truth is painful, Mohan. But you've always stood for justice, no matter the cost. This time is no different. If you turn a blind eye to this, you'll never be able to live with yourself. The choice is yours. Justice… or them."

Mohan's throat tightened as he struggled to breathe. His world had just shattered, and now, standing at the crossroads of justice and family, he had no idea which path to take.

Mohan walked back to his home that night, his steps heavy with the weight of betrayal. His heart pounded, but it wasn't from the physical exertion—it was the unbearable weight of the truth. The ghost's words replayed in his mind: "Your wife and your best friend… they wanted you dead."

The thought alone felt like a blade twisting in his chest. The woman he had loved deeply, the woman with whom he had shared his life, and his friend who had been by his side through thick and thin—they were part of a conspiracy to kill him. He couldn't wrap his mind around it.

As Mohan entered his home, he didn't even look at Geetha. She was in the living room, her face lighting up as she saw him.

"Mohan, you're home late! I was getting worried," she said with concern in her voice. He couldn't respond. His throat tightened, and without a word, he moved past her and went straight to the bedroom, his face blank, his emotions buried deep inside him.

Geetha followed him, confused. "Mohan, are you okay? Did something happen at work?"

He shook his head slightly, avoiding her gaze, unable to even muster a fake smile. "I'm just tired, Geetha. I need some rest."

She looked at him with concern, but nodded. "Alright, you rest. We'll talk in the morning." She kissed his forehead gently, and Mohan's heart broke a little more.

Once Geetha had fallen asleep beside him, Mohan lay awake in the darkness, staring at the ceiling. His mind raced with memories of their love—the times they laughed together, the moments they supported each other through struggles, the deep connection they shared.

But now, those memories felt like ashes in his mouth. He had trusted her completely, believed in their bond. How could she betray me? How could Ramesh betray me? His mind screamed in silent torment.

And then there was the ghost's voice—calm, certain, and unyielding: "There's something between your wife and Ramesh. They wanted you out of the way."

Mohan clenched his fists under the covers, his body rigid with tension. "Why?" he asked himself over and over. "What did I do wrong? Was our love not enough? Did I miss the signs?"

He thought of Ramesh—his closest friend, the man who had shared his struggles and triumphs. How could he have conspired with Geetha? The ghost had said it had proof, but what if it was wrong? What if it was all a terrible misunderstanding?

But the ghost had never misled him before. It had always been his guide, leading him down the path of justice. Yet now, the price of following that path seemed unbearable.

Mohan turned on his side, staring at Geetha's sleeping face. She looked peaceful, unaware of the storm raging inside him. His heart ached as he remembered their early days together—their wedding, the promises they made, the life they had built. How could it all be a lie?

"Did you ever love me, Geetha?" he whispered to himself in the silence of the night. His voice was barely audible, but it echoed loudly in his soul.

The hours dragged on, each one more torturous than the last. The thought of Geetha's and Ramesh's betrayal burned inside him like acid. Was it really true? Could they really have plotted my death?

His mind swung between disbelief and acceptance, each emotion leaving him more drained than the last. "What do I do now?" he asked himself, over and over again. "Do I confront her? Do I trust the ghost? Or do I trust my heart?"

But the hardest question, the one that tortured him the most, was the ghost's ultimatum: "Justice or family?"

Mohan didn't sleep that night. His mind was consumed with memories of happier times, shadowed by the chilling possibility that the two people he loved most in the world had tried to kill him. How do I choose between my duty and my heart?

By the time dawn broke, Mohan felt like a different man—one torn apart by an impossible decision, knowing that whichever path he chose, he would lose something dear to him.

The ghost's words haunted him as much as his own feelings did: "You must choose justice, Mohan. But at what cost?.

In the early hours of the morning, Mohan stumbled upon a pile of documents and papers that the ghost had promised. They were scattered across the table—clear evidence against his wife Geetha and his best friend Ramesh. Each piece of paper felt heavier than the last as he sifted through them, his hands trembling. This day would be the worst day of his life, and deep down, he knew there was no turning back.

He stood for a moment, his heart pounding. "How did it come to this? "he whispered to himself. Every part of him wanted to reject what was in front of him, but the truth was undeniable. Justice had always been his guiding principle, but now, it was threatening to tear his entire world apart.

Mohan made his way to his mother's room, hoping she would understand, hoping she could somehow give him the strength he needed to confront this nightmare. But as he began to explain, Kamala Devi's face hardened with disbelief.

"What are you saying, Mohan?" She asked, her voice rising with every word. "Your wife and Ramesh? Planning to kill you? Have you lost your mind?"

"No, Mummy, I have proof," Mohan insisted, showing her the documents. "I'm sorry, but they conspired against me."

His mother's eyes blazed with anger. "How dare you accuse them of such horrible things? This is your family, your friend! You are blinded by something, Mohan. This is madness!"

In a fit of rage, Kamala Devi began to scold and hit him, tears streaming down her face. "You think fame and power mean more than your family? You've changed! You've become obsessed with your status as a police officer, and now you're ready to destroy the people who love you the most!"

Mohan, fighting back tears of his own, stood there helpless. "Mummy, I swear it's the truth. They tried to kill me… I can't let it go. Justice is everything."

Just then, Geetha, who had overheard the conversation, walked into the room. Her face was as pale as a ghost, her eyes wide with shock. As the weight of Mohan's accusations sank in, she gasped and collapsed, to the floor.

Mohan rushed to her side, his heart torn apart by the sight of his wife lying motionless. But his sense of duty burned within him. He couldn't turn back now.

At that moment, Ramesh arrived, hearing the commotion. "What's going on here?" he asked, his voice filled with concern.

When Kamala Devi told him what Mohan had said, Ramesh was stunned, his face turning pale. "Are you serious, Mohan?" he shouted in disbelief. "You're accusing me of trying to kill you? Your own friend? You've completely lost it!"

Mohan, staring at the ground, felt the overwhelming weight of his decision, but he stood firm. "I have evidence, Ramesh. I'm sorry, but justice must come first, even if it costs me everything."

Ramesh, now furious, yelled at Mohan. "You've changed! You've become so obsessed with your position, your so-called justice, that you're willing to destroy everything just to maintain your name and fame. Is this what being a police officer means to you?"

Mohan's heart ached, but his resolve was unshakable. He picked up his phone and called the police. "I'm sorry, Ramesh. I'm sorry, Geetha. But I can't ignore what's right. I have to do this."

His voice cracked with emotion, but his actions were firm. When the police arrived, Mohan gave the order to arrest both his wife and his friend. His mother cried out, begging him to reconsider, but Mohan closed his eyes, fighting back the tears. "Justice is everything," he whispered to himself. "It always has been."

As the police led Geetha and Ramesh away, the pain in Mohan's chest felt unbearable. He had upheld justice, but at the cost of his family and the people he loved most. The ghost, watching from the shadows, appeared beside him and smiled faintly.

"You made the right choice, Mohan," it said. "Justice isn't easy, but you stayed true to yourself. For that, I congratulate you."

Mohan stood there, numb, wondering if this was truly the price of justice. Yet, even in his despair, he knew he had done what was right.

Sometimes, the hardest choices are the ones that define us. Mohan's journey, though filled with difficult decisions, shows how staying true to one's values is the most powerful thing , no matter the personal cost.

Mohan sat in his empty living room, the once vibrant home now quiet, filled only with the distant hum of city life. His hands trembled as he held an old family photo—a moment frozen in time, capturing the days before the accident, before the dog's eye, before the ghost. His face softened, remembering those days. The picture showed him with his wife, Geetha, his mother, and Ramesh. Back then, they were all smiling, united in love, laughter, and friendship. The photo seemed like a relic from a distant life that now felt impossible to reach.

"We were so happy," Mohan whispered to himself, his voice thick with regret. "Before all of this… before the accident, before justice consumed everything."

He closed his eyes and thought of the dog—the loyal companion that had saved him once, and in a way, had damned him too. Mohan's mind wandered back to that fateful night in the jungle, where he had lost more than just his eye. Since then, everything had changed. The eye, gifted with the ability to see the supernatural, had brought him power, wealth, and success. But with each triumph, he had lost a piece of his soul.

He had become Chief of Police, respected, admired. Yet, with every case he solved, with every promotion he earned, something far more important slipped away— his family, his happiness, his peace.

"I thought I had everything," Mohan muttered, rubbing his temples as if to stave off the weight of his thoughts. "Name, position, wealth, success. But… what have I really gained?"

His mind raced back to the ghost—the silent guide that had appeared when Mohan needed it most. The ghost had promised him justice, had promised him that with its help, he could become the man he always wanted to be. And Mohan had believed it. The ghost had shown him the hidden truths behind every crime, every mystery. But what the ghost hadn't revealed was the cost—how much he'd have to sacrifice in the name of justice.

"Justice…" Mohan said aloud, shaking his head. "What does it even mean anymore? Is it worth losing everything? My family? My friend? My happiness?"

The realization that his wife and best friend had conspired to kill him haunted him, but so did the consequences of his actions. He had arrested them, upheld justice as the ghost had guided him to do. But in doing so, he had shattered the very foundation of his life. His mother had turned against him. Geetha and Ramesh, the two people he loved most, were now behind bars. And for what? Justice? Or a twisted sense of duty that had left him utterly alone?

The ghost appeared again, as it often did when Mohan's thoughts became too heavy to bear. This time, however, the ghost didn't offer words of encouragement or praise. It simply stood there, watching, silent.

Mohan looked at it, his eyes filled with frustration and sorrow. "You told me justice was everything. You said I would find peace, that I would be happy if I followed the path of justice. But look at me now. I'm empty. Alone. Was this really the right path?"

The ghost's pale eyes glimmered, and for a moment, it seemed almost human. "Justice," it finally spoke, its voice low and haunting, "is not meant to bring happiness. Justice is meant to restore balance. And balance, Mohan, always comes with a cost. You knew this from the beginning."

Mohan's heart ached, the words cutting deep. "But the cost was too high," he replied, his voice cracking. "I've lost everything. My family hates me. I can't even bear to look at my own wife. My best friend betrayed me. And now... now, I don't know who I am anymore."

The ghost stepped closer, its spectral form flickering in the dim light of the room. "You are a man of justice. That is who you are. You did what needed to be done. Your wife and friend betrayed you. Should you have ignored that for the sake of your own happiness? Should you have let injustice continue simply because it hurt to confront it?"

Mohan felt his breath hitch in his chest. He didn't know how to answer that. Part of him wanted to scream yes—that he should have turned a blind eye, kept his family intact, and chosen love over justice. But another part of him knew the truth. He had always been a man of principle. He had always believed in doing what was right, even when it hurt.

Yet, sitting there now, surrounded by the emptiness of his once happy home, he couldn't help but feel like he had lost something far more valuable than justice had given him.

"Maybe justice isn't everything," Mohan murmured, almost to himself. "Maybe I was wrong to think it could replace love, family, and happiness."

The ghost looked at him with a strange intensity. "Justice and happiness do not always walk hand in hand, Mohan. But you must decide what kind of man you want to be. A man who sacrifices for what is right, or a man who turns away from truth to hold onto illusions."

Mohan dropped his head into his hands, the weight of the decision crushing him. He had chosen justice, yes, but had it been worth it? In the end, he had everything society valued— power, authority, respect. But inside, he felt more broken than ever.

"Maybe I'm not as strong as I thought," he whispered, tears welling up in his eyes. "Maybe… I wasn't ready to pay the price of justice. "The ghost faded into the shadows, leaving Mohan alone once more, a man torn between duty and the life he wished he still had.

CHAPTER 11

Mohan sat in his jeep, parked under the dim streetlights on a quiet night. He was speaking on the phone with one of his subordinates, giving instructions about a recent case. His mind was sharp, focused on his duties as the chief of police. The weight of the decisions he had made recently hung in the background, but for now, work was his escape.

Suddenly, out of the corner of his eye, he saw the familiar figure of the ghost appear. It hovered at a distance, silent but evidently disturbed. Mohan finished his conversation on the phone, his attention now fully on the ghost. He had grown accustomed to these encounters, but there was something unsettling in the ghost's demeanour tonight.

"What is it this time?" Mohan asked, his voice tinged with impatience.

The ghost hovered closer, its voice low and serious. "This matter... it's more serious than anything we've ever faced in your accident case"

Mohan's brow furrowed, the frustration he had been holding back now creeping into his tone.

"More serious? I've already sent my cousin, my wife, and my best friend to jail. Who else could possibly be involved? Who am I supposed to send to jail this time?"

The ghost paused, its face clouded with sorrow. "This time, Mohan... it will be even more torturous for you."

Mohan felt a chill run down his spine. He had grown accustomed to the ghost's cryptic warnings, but something about this one felt different. "Torturous? Who? "he demanded, the tension in his voice rising.

The ghost's eyes glimmered with sorrow as it whispered, "It's not a 'he' this time. It's a 'she.'"

Mohan's heart skipped a beat. His mind raced through the possibilities. "She? Who are you talking about?" His voice was sharp, almost angry now.

The ghost hesitated for a brief moment before uttering the words Mohan never expected to hear. "Your mother."

The world seemed to stand still. Mohan's hands tightened on the steering wheel, his knuckles turning white. "My mother?" he echoed, disbelief and fury clashing within him. "What are you saying?"

The ghost floated closer, its voice urgent. "Your mother was involved in the accident. She had her reasons, but she was part of the plan"

Before the ghost could finish, Mohan's rage exploded. "Enough!" he roared. "I don't want to hear any more of your lies!" His heart pounded in his chest, and his breath came in ragged gasps. The thought that his own mother, the woman who had raised him, could be part of the conspiracy to kill him was too much to bear.

Without another word, Mohan slammed his foot on the gas pedal, and the jeep roared to life. The tires screeched as he sped down the empty road, trying to outrun the ghost and its devastating revelations. "I won't listen to this!" he shouted into the wind.

The ghost followed him, gliding effortlessly through the air beside the speeding jeep, its voice echoing in the night. "Mohan! Stop! Listen to me! You need to know the truth!" But Mohan wasn't ready to listen. His mind was a storm of emotions—anger, betrayal, confusion. How could his own mother be involved? His family had already been shattered by the truth about his cousin, wife, and friend. He couldn't bear the thought of losing her too.

As he pushed the jeep to its limits, the vehicle began to sputter. Suddenly, without warning, the jeep slowed down and came to a complete stop, its engine dead. Mohan cursed under his breath and tried to restart it, but no matter how hard he turned the key, the engine wouldn't respond.

He slammed his fist on the steering wheel in frustration, then got out of the jeep, looking around. The night was terribly quiet, the wind howling softly through the trees. A sense of dread washed over him as he spotted an old church nearby, its silhouette barely visible in the moonlight. The clouds overhead churned ominously, and the distant rumble of thunder signalled an approaching storm.

With no other options and the weather worsening, Mohan decided to seek shelter in the church. He trudged toward it, glancing behind him as the ghost continued to follow at a distance, still pleading with him to listen.

"Mohan, please!" the ghost called out, its voice now more desperate than before. "This is the truth. You have to face it!" But Mohan ignored the ghost, his mind in turmoil. He pushed open the heavy wooden doors of the church and stepped inside. The interior was cold, dark, and filled with an overwhelming sense of stillness. The pews were empty, and the air smelled faintly of incense and old wood.

Mohan sat down heavily in one of the pews, burying his face in his hands. His heart was pounding, and his thoughts raced in circles. Could it really be true? Could his own mother, the one person he had thought he could still trust, have been involved in the plot to kill him?

Outside the church, the ghost hovered near the entrance, unable to come any closer. It paced back and forth in the dark, its translucent form flickering with agitation. The spectral figure seemed to pulse with frustration as it watched Mohan ignore its warnings.

"Mohan!" the ghost's voice cut through the stillness like a sharp wind. "Come out! You must listen to me! You don't understand what you're dealing with!"

But Mohan, lost in his thoughts, didn't respond. His mind was reeling. Could it really be true? Could his mother—the woman who had loved and raised him, the one person he had trusted implicitly—have been involved in the plan to kill him? He couldn't fathom it, and yet, the ghost had been right about everything else. His cousin, his wife, his best friend—all of them had betrayed him, and each time, the ghost had warned him. Each time, it had led him to the truth.

"Mohan! You don't know the full story!" the ghost shouted, its voice more insistent now. "I can give you the evidence you need, but you must come out! You have to listen!"

Mohan clenched his fists, the leather of his gloves creaking under the pressure. He had heard enough. The ghost had already taken so much from him—his trust in the people he loved, his sense of safety, his happiness. Now, it wanted to take his mother too?

The ghost grew more frantic as it watched Mohan's silent defiance. Its voice cracked with desperation. "Mohan, please! I can't enter the church. It's forbidden for me. I can't meet where you are now! You have to come out, or you'll never know the whole truth!"

The church, sacred and untouchable, was a place the ghost could not cross into. Its anger was palpable as it hovered just beyond the threshold, its form flickering like a dying flame.

Inside, Mohan sat motionless, staring at the altar ahead, his mind a whirlwind of emotions. He wanted to scream, to release the fury and grief that had built up inside him. But instead, he remained silent, locked in a battle with his own thoughts.

"You think you know everything," the ghost continued from outside, its voice now almost pleading. "But you don't! The accident, your mother's role—it's more complicated than you realize. She didn't want to harm you, Mohan. You have to understand why she did what she did. I have the evidence, but I can't give it to you if you stay inside. You need to trust me one last time."

Trust? How could he trust the ghost again? How could he trust anyone? Everyone he had once loved, everyone he had relied on, had been exposed as a traitor. His wife, his best friend, his cousin—they were all gone, locked away in prison because of this relentless pursuit of justice. Now, the ghost was telling him that his mother, the last remaining pillar in his crumbling world, was guilty too.

Mohan's heart ached with confusion. He had always prided himself on being a man of justice, on doing what was right no matter the cost. But at what point did the cost become too high? Was justice worth losing everything—his family, his peace, his very sanity?

"Mohan!" The ghost's voice rose, trembling with a mix of anger and fear. "You don't know what you're rejecting. If you don't come out, you'll be lost forever. I'm trying to save you from making another mistake!"

Mohan looked up, his gaze wandering across the stained-glass windows that lined the walls of the church. The coloured light cast long, distorted shadows on the floor, creating a kaleidoscope of reds and blues that danced around the empty pews. It was peaceful here, far removed from the madness outside. He longed for the peace to stay, to let the church swallow him whole, away from the ghost's incessant demands, away from the brutal truths that had torn his life apart.

But even as he tried to block out the ghost's voice, a part of him wondered if he was making a mistake. The ghost had been right before. Every time it had led him down the path of justice, it had been painful, but it had been the truth. Could he really turn away from that now?

The ghost, seeing no response from Mohan, grew even more frantic. Its form flickered violently, and it let out a piercing cry. "I've shown you the truth every time, Mohan! You can't stop now. Don't you want justice for yourself, for your family? Your mother is involved, but you need to know why! You must decide—will you choose justice or family again?"

Mohan flinched at the words. The eternal question. Justice or family. Every time, he had chosen justice. Every time, it had cost him more than he had anticipated. Now, he was standing on the edge once again, forced to choose between knowing the truth and preserving what little remained of his shattered world.

The rain began to fall outside, heavy drops pounding against the church's roof like a drumbeat, adding to the sense of impending doom. Mohan's heart thudded in his chest, matching the rhythm of the storm.

He closed his eyes, taking a deep breath, and for the first time that night, he allowed himself to feel the full weight of his exhaustion. The burden of being the one to uphold justice had drained him. He had once thought of himself as the happiest man alive, proud of his duty and accomplishments. Now, that man felt like a stranger.

The ghost's voice softened. "You can still walk away, Mohan. But if you do, you'll never truly know what happened. You'll always wonder. Do you really want to live with that uncertainty? Come out, and I'll give you the answers you seek."

Mohan sat slumped in the pew, his hands covering his face as his tears quietly fell. The weight of everything was suffocating him—the ghost's revelations, the arrest of his family, and now the unbearable silence of the empty church. The ghost, after a few more futile attempts to call him out, had vanished into the night, leaving Mohan alone with his tormented thoughts.

The sound of footsteps echoed softly through the church, but Mohan, lost in his grief, didn't notice. It wasn't until the voice of an older man broke the silence that Mohan looked up.

"My son, are you alright?" came the gentle voice of the priest. Mohan's swollen eyes met the gaze of the priest standing before him. He had a kind face, with weathered lines of experience etched into his skin. There was something familiar about him, though Mohan couldn't place it immediately.

"Do I know you?" Mohan asked, his voice hoarse from crying.

The priest smiled softly. "You may not remember, but I remember you very well. I was the doctor who treated you after your accident in the jungle. Back then, I worked in a small hospital. After my retirement, I found a different calling, and now I serve as a priest here."

Mohan's eyes widened in surprise. "You... treated me?" He paused, thinking back to those hazy days after the accident. "I owe you my life."

The priest waved his hand dismissively, his smile gentle. "No, my son. I only did what I could. But seeing you here now, in this state, breaks my heart. Why are you so troubled? What brings you to this place tonight?" Mohan hesitated. He was drowning in his own torment, but he wasn't sure if he could share the dark burden he carried. His instinct was to remain silent, but there was something about the priest's presence that made him feel he could trust him.

"I… it's complicated," Mohan finally said, looking away. "I don't even know where to begin."

The priest sat beside him, patient and calm. "Take your time, my son. The house of God is a place of refuge. Whatever burdens you carry, you don't have to carry them alone. You can tell me what troubles your soul."

Mohan sighed, his heart heavy with indecision. The weight of the ghost's accusations felt unbearable, but he didn't know if he could speak of them. After several moments of silence, he began slowly, each word feeling like a stone in his throat.

"I sent my cousin, my best friend, and my wife to prison," Mohan admitted, his voice barely above a whisper. "They were part of a conspiracy to kill me."

The priest's brow furrowed in disbelief. "Your family? Your friend? Surely, that can't be true."

Mohan nodded solemnly, his gaze dropping to the floor. "I have evidence. They tampered with my jeep, caused the accident. I trusted them, and they betrayed me."

The priest leaned forward, his expression full of concern. "Mohan, I was there when you were unconscious after the accident. I saw how your family took care of you. Your wife, your friend— they were by your side constantly. They never left you. How can you believe that they would want to harm you?"

Mohan shook his head, his voice cracking as he spoke. "I didn't want to believe it either, but I've seen the evidence with my own eyes. They were involved. They wanted me dead."

The priest's face softened, a mix of sorrow and concern in his eyes. "And who gave you this evidence, Mohan? Who convinced you that the people who love you would do such a terrible thing?"

Mohan hesitated, the familiar feeling of doubt creeping into his mind. He had always trusted the ghost's guidance, but now, sitting in the church, surrounded by the stillness of sacred walls, everything felt more uncertain.

"It was a friend of mine," Mohan replied carefully. "Someone I trust.

"The priest's eyes narrowed slightly. "A friend, you say? And yet you won't even speak his name here, in the house of God? Mohan, if this friend truly sought justice, why the secrecy?"

Mohan's chest tightened. He hadn't thought of it that way. The ghost had always been elusive, giving him truth but also leaving behind questions. Now, faced with the priest's gentle but probing questions, Mohan found himself at a crossroads. He had always prided himself on being just, but now the lines between truth and manipulation seemed blurred.

The priest placed a hand on Mohan's shoulder, his touch firm yet compassionate. "My son, this is the house of God. In this place, there can be no lies, no secrets. You must confess everything if you are to find peace. Who is this 'friend' you speak of, the one who has given you this so-called evidence?"

Mohan stared at the ground, his mind racing. How could he explain the ghost to the priest? How could he tell him that it wasn't a living person, but a restless spirit, that had led him to these terrible conclusions? He had made a vow not to reveal the ghost's identity, but here, in this sacred space, that vow felt like a burden.

The priest's voice was calm but insistent. "You cannot hide the truth here, Mohan. If you are seeking forgiveness, if you are seeking clarity, you must be honest with yourself and with God. Who is this friend?"

Mohan's hands trembled. "I… I can't say," he stammered, his voice weak. "I made a promise. An agreement."

The priest frowned, his eyes filled with both disappointment and understanding. "Mohan, agreements made in darkness will only lead to more darkness. If this friend is truly guiding you toward justice, why must his name be hidden? You are in the house of God now, where only the truth will set you free."

Mohan felt trapped. The priest's words rang true, but the ghost had always been clear—its help came at the price of secrecy. But now, more than ever, Mohan felt the weight of doubt pressing down on him. What if the ghost was wrong? What if he had been led astray by something other than justice?

The priest's gaze softened, and he leaned closer, his voice a whisper. "I can see the pain in your heart, my son. Whatever choices you've made, you can still make things right. But you must start by facing the truth. Tell me everything."

Mohan's mind spun with confusion. Should he tell the priest about the ghost? Should he reveal the full extent of what had happened, the choices he had made, and the consequences he now faced?

Tears welled up in Mohan's eyes again, and he found himself sinking further into the pew, overwhelmed by the enormity of his situation. He had fought for justice his entire life, but now he wasn't sure what justice even meant anymore. The father's words echoed in his mind ,"agreements made in darkness"—and he wondered if he had unknowingly walked a path of darkness all along.

But he couldn't find the words to speak, to confess fully. All he could do was sit there, weighed down by the unbearable burden of doubt and regret, as the priest waited patiently beside him.

"Mohan," the priest said gently, "if you want to find peace, you must tell me everything. There is no judgment here, only a desire to help you. What is it that burdens your soul?'

Mohan hesitated, his throat tightening as he thought about the strange and otherworldly secret he had kept for so long. After a few moments of silence, he finally spoke.

"Father, my friend… the one who's been guiding me through all this…"Mohan paused, gathering his courage. "It's not a person. It's a ghost."

The father blinked, clearly taken aback. He leaned back slightly, trying to process what Mohan had just said. "A ghost?" the father repeated slowly, his voice cautious. "How did you become friends with a ghost?''

Mohan sighed, feeling the weight of the strange tale that he was about to unfold.

"It all started after my accident. You might not believe me, but when I woke up, I could see things—things that others couldn't. I could see the ghost because…" Mohan looked the father directly in the eyes. "Because of my dog's eye. When you treated me after the accident, you gave me my dog's eye to save my life."

The father's eyes widened with realization. "Your dog's eye?" he whispered, the words barely escaping his lips. He covered his mouth for a moment, clearly shaken. "I… I remember now. That night, in the hospital, I made a decision. Your injuries were severe, and you would've lost your sight completely. I had no other option. Your dog had died in the accident, and in a desperate attempt to save you, I gave you its eye. It was a medical procedure that should never have been done… but you were dying, and I—"

The father stopped, guilt filling his voice as he recalled that fateful decision.

"It's alright, Father," Mohan interrupted, sensing the father's distress. "You saved my life. I don't hold it against you. And because of that eye… I gained something else. The ghost—it helped me."

The father, still trying to come to terms with his actions, shook his head slowly. "Mohan, this ghost you speak of… how did it help you? How did you come to trust it?"

Mohan leaned forward, his voice filled with a strange mix of awe and certainty. "It showed me things—truths about the people around me. It guided me, helped me expose corruption, and led me back to my job. Because of it, I regained my name, my position, my wealth. Everything I am today, I owe to this ghost. It has never led me astray."

The father frowned, deep concern clouding his face. "Mohan, no ghost—no matter how it appears—can guide a person to good. Ghosts are remnants of the dead, restless spirits. They may pretend to help, but their motives are never pure. This ghost may have given you success, but at what cost?"

Mohan shook his head, defending the spirit that had been his companion through the darkest times. "No, Father, you don't understand. This ghost has only ever pushed me toward justice. It made sure I held people accountable, even when it was painful. It helped me do what was right."

The father sighed deeply, his voice soft but firm. "Mohan, no ghost—good or bad—can bring true justice. They are bound by the darkness of their existence. You think it's helping you, but look at the price you've paid. You've lost your family, your happiness, and now… you're here, crying in this church. Do you really believe that's the work of a friend?"

Mohan fell silent at the father's words, his mind racing. The father's question hung in the air, impossible to ignore. "Are you happy, Mohan?" the father asked gently. "Despite all the success you've gained, all the power and fame… are you truly at peace?"

Mohan didn't answer right away. He looked down at his hands, still trembling from the weight of the decisions he had made. "No," he admitted at last, his voice barely a whisper. "I'm not happy. I've lost the people I care about. I don't know what's true anymore."

The father nodded, understanding the depth of Mohan's turmoil. "That's because ghosts—no matter how they present themselves—are not capable of bringing peace. They thrive on chaos, on confusion. They pull you away from what truly matters. And now, Mohan, look at what it has done. You've lost the love of your family, the most precious thing a man can have. You're sitting here, broken and alone."

Mohan's throat tightened and tears threatened to fall again. "But Father… this ghost has done so much for me. It gave me everything I have."

The father looked at him with kind but serious eyes. "Mohan, the ghost may have given you things, but it has taken even more. It has taken the love of your family, the joy you once had, the real happiness of being surrounded by people who care for you. Can you not see? You've traded your soul's peace for temporary success. Was it worth it?"

Mohan sat in silence, the truth of the father's words finally sinking in. He felt the crushing weight of realization, a pain deeper than any he had felt before. "No," he whispered, his voice cracking. "It wasn't worth it. I'm… I'm not happy. I'm not happy at all."

The father leaned closer, his voice gentle but firm. "Mohan, it's not too late. You must confront this ghost. You must ask it why it has led you down this path. Only then will you begin to understand. But remember this—no ghost, no matter how helpful it may seem, is a friend. It thrives on darkness, and it has taken you away from the light."

Mohan looked up, his eyes filled with both fear and determination. "What should I do, Father? How do I confront it?"

The father stood up and walked toward the altar, returning with a small wooden cross. He handed it to Mohan, his expression solemn. "Take this with you, my son. This is no ordinary task. You are dealing with a force that has manipulated your heart and soul. You must protect yourself."

Mohan took the cross, feeling its weight in his hand. "Thank you, Father." The father smiled, though his eyes still carried the burden of concern. "I once treated you physically, Mohan. Now, it's time to treat you spiritually. Go, and confront this spirit. But remember, you walk in the light of God. No ghost can take that from you if you stay true to the path."

Mohan nodded, feeling a renewed sense of purpose. The cross in his hand felt like a lifeline, a guide in the storm that had consumed his life. He stood, thanked the father once more, and turned to leave the church.

As he stepped out into the night, the wind howled around him, and Mohan felt the presence of the ghost lingering somewhere in the shadows. But this time, he was ready to face it. He had questions that needed answers— truths that needed to be uncovered. And with the father's words echoing in his mind, Mohan knew that this confrontation would determine the course of the rest of his life.

CHAPTER 12

Mohan stepped out of the church, clutching the cross the father had given him. The air was cool and heavy, as though the night itself was waiting for something to unfold. He walked toward his jeep, still parked where it had mysteriously stopped earlier. "Why did it stop here?" Mohan muttered to himself, glancing up at the dark church behind him. "Was it some sign from God?"

He climbed into the driver's seat, fully expecting the engine to remain silent as it had before. But this time, when he turned the key, the jeep roared to life effortlessly. Mohan's eyes widened in surprise.

"What in the world?" he whispered. "It starts now? Why did it stop in front of the church in the first place?"

As he drove down the road, a sense of unease crept into his mind. He had revealed everything to the father, and while that had brought him some peace, he knew the ghost would not be pleased. Still, he drove on, the trees whipping past as he pushed the jeep faster.

Not more than a mile later, the ghost appeared in the middle of the road, its pale figure glowing against the darkness. Mohan hit the brakes hard, his heart pounding in his chest as the jeep screeched to a halt.

The ghost hovered before him, its expression contorted with rage. "Mohan!" it hissed. "Have you revealed everything to the father?"

Mohan stepped out of the jeep, gripping the cross tightly in his hand. "I had no choice," he said, his voice steady. "In the house of God, I couldn't hide the truth. The father urged me to confess, and I did."

The ghost's eyes narrowed, its voice seething with anger. "You've broken our agreement, Mohan. You've done wrong !"

Mohan shook his head, his resolve unshaken.

"You helped me, yes, but you've taken away my happiness. You guided me down a path that led me to destroy my own family. Why? Why would you do that?"

The ghost's anger turned into a cold, strange laugh, sending chills down Mohan's spine. "Are you suffering, Mohan? Are you filled with regret and pain?"

Mohan felt his stomach churn as he replied softly, "Yes... I am."

The ghost's grin widened with malevolent delight. "Good. That's exactly what I wanted."

Mohan's heart dropped. "What? What do you mean?" he asked, his voice rising with shock.

The ghost floated closer, its voice taunting.

"I wanted to see you suffer, Mohan. I wanted to take away everything that mattered to you. Your cousin, your wife, your friend—they were innocent. They loved you deeply."

Mohan staggered backward, his mind reeling. "No…" he whispered. "No, that's not possible. You gave me the evidence. You showed me they conspired to kill me!"

The ghost's laughter grew darker, more sinister "The evidence? Oh, Mohan… that was all fake. Every bit of it. I fabricated it all, just to lead you astray."

Mohan felt a cold sweat break out on his forehead. His hands trembled as the weight of the ghost's confession sank in. "You lied to me… you made me send the people I loved to prison for crimes they didn't commit."

The ghost's expression twisted with sadistic glee. "Yes. And now, look at you. Alone, Broken. Full of regret."

Mohan's anger flared, burning through his grief. "Why? Why did you do this to me? What did I ever do to you?"

The ghost's face contorted with rage at Mohan's question. "You still don't remember, do you?" it snarled. "You, Mohan, are the one who did me wrong. You think you're the victim, but you're the reason I'm like this."

Mohan stared at the ghost, confused and horrified. "What are you talking about? What wrong did I do to you?"

The ghost drifted closer, its voice dripping with bitterness. "Remember the night of your accident, Mohan? In the jungle, your jeep crashed into a car."

Mohan nodded slowly, his mind racing. "Yes… but what does that have to do with you?"

The ghost's eyes blazed with anger. "I was the driver of that car."

Mohan froze, the memory of the accident flooding back. He had never thought much about the other vehicle—his own injuries had consumed his thoughts. But now, hearing this revelation, his heart began to pound with dread. The ghost's voice trembled with rage.

"After the accident, the rescue team came for you. They saved you because you were a police officer. But me? I was just a poor driver. They left me behind, injured and dying. I cried out for help, but no one came. No one cared."

Mohan's breath caught in his throat. "You... you were the driver? But... I didn't know..."

The ghost's fury boiled over. "Of course, you didn't! You were too busy being saved, while I lay there, suffering, alone, until I died. No one even bothered to look for me. And you went on with your life, your reputation intact, while I was forgotten."

Mohan staggered back, overwhelmed by the weight of the ghost's words. His mind spun with the realization that the father had been right all along. "Oh, God..." he whispered. "I didn't know. I didn't realize..."

The ghost glared at him, its rage still burning.

"You didn't realize. That's why I came back. To make you suffer as I suffered. To take everything from you, the way everything was taken from me."

Mohan was speechless, his guilt consuming him. He had never imagined that the accident that nearly took his life had such a dark consequence for another.

"I… I'm sorry," Mohan choked out, tears welling in his eyes. "If I had known, I would have done something. I didn't mean for this to happen."

The ghost's expression softened, but only for a moment. "It's too late for apologies, Mohan. What's done is done. You took everything from me, and now I've taken everything from you."

Mohan collapsed to his knees, the weight of his actions crashing down on him. "I… I never meant for this. I never wanted any of this…"

 The ghost hovered above him, its form flickering in the dark night. "You wanted success, power, justice. But in the end, you lost what truly mattered."

Mohan's tears fell freely now, the cross still clutched in his trembling hands. "What do I do now?" he asked, his voice broken and desperate. "How do I fix this?"

The ghost remained silent, its anger fading into something more sorrowful. "You can't fix the past, Mohan. But you can live with the truth. That's all you have left now."

Mohan stood frozen, staring at the ghost, his mind reeling. He gripped the cross tighter, trying to make sense of what he had just heard. His voice was shaky when he finally spoke.

"How am I responsible for your death?" Mohan asked, his eyes pleading for answers. "It was an accident. I didn't plan to harm you."

The ghost's expression twisted into one of bitter anger. Its voice was low, but each word carried venom.

"Yes, it was an accident. But for you, there was rescue. For me, there was nothing-no one. And you ask why?" The ghost's pale figure flickered, moving closer. "Why was there a team to save you, but no one for me?"

Mohan shook his head, trying to explain. "I was unconscious after the accident. I didn't know what had happened. I couldn't help you... I didn't even know you were there!"

The ghost's eyes flared with rage. "You didn't know?" it spat. "Let me tell you what happened after you were pulled to safety. While you lay there, unconscious but alive, I was left in the middle of that dark jungle. I was injured, unable to move. I shouted for help, but no one came. No one!"

Mohan felt a cold dread creep up his spine as the ghost's voice trembled with a mixture of fury and sorrow.

"Do you know what it's like, Mohan?" the ghost continued, its voice breaking. "To lie there, abandoned, in agony? And then, as the night grew darker, the animals of the jungle came for me. They dragged me deeper into the wilderness." The ghost paused, its eyes gleaming with a haunting intensity. "They started to eat me... while I was still alive."

Mohan's heart pounded in his chest. He could hardly breathe, the horror of the ghost's words sinking in like a knife. "Oh God... "

"You don't know the pain I endured that night!" the ghost screamed, cutting him off. "And now you stand here, telling me you didn't do anything wrong! That you didn't even know?!"

Mohan's voice faltered guilt and fear crashing over him. "I didn't know... I swear, I didn't know."

The ghost's anger softened for a brief moment, replaced by a deep sadness. "Even after I died, there was no peace. No funeral. No proper rites. I was an orphan, Mohan, with no one to care for me, no one to search for my body. Not even the police bothered to investigate. I was forgotten. Left to rot."

Mohan could barely speak as the weight of the ghost's suffering pressed down on him. "I... I'm sorry," he whispered, his voice trembling. "I didn't know. If I had-"

"It's too late for your apologies!" the ghost bellowed, its voice echoing through the still night. "I became a ghost because of you! From your neglect, your ignorance! And now I seek my revenge on all of humanity, but especially on you, Mohan. It's you I want."

Mohan's hands trembled as he looked into the ghost's eyes. "What do you want from me?"

The ghost's face twisted into a mocking smile. "I wanted to kill you when I first found you, Mohan. But then I realized that death would be too easy for you. I wanted you to suffer instead. To endure a life worse than death." The ghost's laughter was cold and hollow as it continued. "That's why I made sure your loved ones were taken from you. Your cousin, your wife, your friend- they are all in prison because of me. I fed you lies, and you believed them. You destroyed your own happiness."

Mohan felt a wave of nausea as the truth of the ghost's words hit him like a blow. "You... you did all of this?"

The ghost nodded slowly. "Yes. And it's only the beginning. You will suffer more, Mohan. Much more. Only then I will be satisfied."

Mohan's voice was barely a whisper as he asked, "How did you find me? How did you even know about me?" The ghost's smile grew darker. "Ah... I must thank the dog's eye for that. It was through your dog's eye that I was able to see you, to follow you. From the moment you first looked at me through your dog's gaze, I knew I had found the man responsible for my suffering."

Mohan's eyes widened in realization. "The dog's eye..." he muttered, his mind racing. "I have to remove it."

But before Mohan could make any further plans, the ghost's voice dropped to a deadly whisper. "If you even think about removing that eye, Mohan, I will kill you. Not just you, but your entire family." The ghost's face twisted with fury. "Don't test me."

Mohan's heart raced as the ghost began to fade, its figure dissolving into the dark night. "Remember my words, Mohan. You have only just begun to suffer."

And with that, the ghost was gone.

Mohan stood alone in the cold night, his mind swirling with fear and guilt. He needed help, There was only one person he could turn to now. "I have to go back to the father," Mohan whispered to himself, his voice shaky but determined.

With a heavy heart, he climbed back into his jeep and began the drive back to the church. "I have to go back to the father," Mohan whispered to himself, With a heavy heart, he climbed back into his jeep and began the drive back to the church.

Mohan's mind was racing as he drove back toward the church. His hands gripped the steering wheel tightly, and the ghost's parting words echoed in his ears.

"How did this happen?" he muttered to himself, his voice barely audible over the hum of the jeep's engine. "How did I get caught in this trap?"

He thought back to the accident in the jungle, replaying the moments in his mind. He hadn't known, hadn't been conscious, and yet, the ghost blamed him for its death. But how could he have known? How was he responsible?

"I didn't do anything wrong," he said, his voice shaky. "It was an accident. I was unconscious. How could I be responsible for what happened to the ghost?"

But the ghost's voice haunted him, relentless and angry. "It was an accident for you, but for me, it was a nightmare. No rescue, no one to help me… left to die in agony. You, Mohan, had the world come to your aid. I had no one."

Mohan gritted his teeth, trying to shut out the memories. "I didn't know!" he shouted into the empty air. "I didn't know you were there!"

But deep down, the guilt gnawed at him. He had lived while the ghost had suffered, abandoned in the jungle. The more he thought about it, the heavier the weight on his chest became.

"The father was right," Mohan whispered. "This is all so much bigger than me. I need to go back to him."

As the church came into view, Mohan parked the jeep outside and hurried toward the entrance, his thoughts in turmoil. He pushed open the heavy doors, feeling the calmness of the sacred space settle over him, though his heart was still pounding.

He found the father in the same place he had left him, sitting quietly, seemingly deep in thought. The father looked up as Mohan approached, his eyes filled with a mixture of concern and understanding. "Mohan," the father said gently, "you've returned."

Mohan nodded, his voice trembling. "I need your help, father. The ghost… it spoke to me. It's after me because of something that happened the night of my accident."

The father gestured for Mohan to sit, his eyes never leaving Mohan's face. "Tell me everything, my son."

Mohan sat down heavily, recounting every word of the ghost's terrifying confession. How it had been left to die in the jungle, how it had suffered at the hands of wild animals, and how its death had gone unnoticed, while Mohan had been rescued.

When Mohan finished, the father sighed deeply, his face etched with sympathy. "This ghost is filled with vengeance, Mohan. It believes you are responsible for its suffering, and it's using that anger to punish you."

Mohan looked at the father, desperation in his eyes. "But how could I have known? I was unconscious… I didn't leave it to die on purpose!"

The father placed a comforting hand on Mohan's shoulder. "The ghost's suffering has twisted its soul, Mohan. It can no longer see the difference between accident and intent. It sees only its pain, and it wants you to feel the same."

Mohan swallowed hard, his throat tight. "I don't know what to do. It said it would kill me and my family if I tried to remove the dog's eye. But I can't keep living like this, with this curse over my head."

The father nodded slowly. "You are trapped, Mohan. But there is a way forward, though it will not be easy."

Mohan leaned in, desperate for answers. "What do I need to do?"

The father's voice was calm but firm. "You must confront the ghost again. This time, not with anger, but with compassion. You must help it find peace. That's the only way to break the curse."

Mohan's eyes widened in disbelief. "Confront it? After everything it's done to me?"

The father nodded. "Yes, Mohan. The ghost's vengeance is born from its pain. If you can help it find closure, perhaps it will let go of its anger. But you must be careful. This is a delicate path, and the ghost will not give up its desire for revenge easily."

Mohan hesitated, fear bubbling up inside him. "What if it refuses? What if it still wants to make me suffer?"

The father handed Mohan the cross once again, his gaze steady. "That's why you must go prepared, my son. You have the strength within you. You must face the darkness to find the light."

Mohan looked down at the cross in his hands, feeling its weight. He had no idea how he was going to face the ghost again, but he knew he had no choice. His fate—and the fate of his family—depended on it.

"I'll do it," he whispered, more to himself than to the father. "I'll face the ghost one last time."

The father's eyes softened as he spoke one final blessing over Mohan. "Go with courage, Mohan. You are not alone in this. Have faith, and you will find the strength to set things right."

Mohan stood up, gripping the cross tightly. He felt the weight of the father's words, and though fear still lingered in his heart, something else began to grow—a small flicker of hope.

Mohan stepped out of the church, the night air heavy with anticipation. He could feel the presence of the ghost before he even saw it. As he reached the gate, there it was, waiting—its form terribly still, glowing faintly against the darkness.

His breath caught in his throat as he called out, "Father!"

The door of the church creaked open, and the father hurried out, concern etched on his face. "What is it, Mohan?"

Mohan pointed toward the gate. "The ghost... it's right there, waiting for me."

The father looked where Mohan was pointing, his eyes scanning the darkness. "I see nothing, my son," he said calmly. "Are you certain?"

Mohan nodded vigorously, fear creeping into his voice. "It's there, Father. It's standing right in front of us. I can see it."

The father stepped forward, placing a steady hand on Mohan's shoulder. "Remember, Mohan, the spirit may reveal itself to you alone because it harbours its grievances against you. But you must try to speak to it, to reach its heart. This is your task."

Mohan swallowed hard, taking a step toward the ghost. "I... I want to talk to you," he began, his voice trembling slightly. "Please, listen to me."

The ghost's form flickered, its expression cold and distant. Its voice was low, a chilling whisper that only Mohan could hear. "Talk? You think words can undo the pain, Mohan? After everything you've done?"

Mohan felt a knot tighten in his stomach. "I know I've hurt you. I know you suffered because of me, but I didn't mean for any of this to happen. I'm here to make things right."

The ghost's eyes flared with anger. "Make things right? You can't undo my death! You lived, and I was left to rot, forgotten in the jungle. You have no idea what I went through."

Mohan's hands tightened around the cross the father had given him. "I know I can't bring you back, but I don't want this anger to consume both of us. Please… let me help you find peace."

But the ghost only laughed, a hollow, echoing sound that chilled Mohan to the bone. "You think peace can be found so easily? I have haunted you, made you suffer, and I am not done yet. You deserve more pain, more loss."

Mohan turned to the father, his face pale. "It's not listening, Father. It still wants to hurt me." The father stepped closer, his voice calm yet commanding. "Spirit, you hold onto your anger, but what good has it brought you? You have caused suffering, yes, but your soul remains trapped in this world. The peace you seek can only be found in forgiveness."

The ghost hissed, its form rippling as though the father's words had struck it. "Forgiveness? What do you know of my suffering, priest?"

The father spoke firmly, his eyes focused on the empty space where the ghost stood. "I know that your soul is restless, bound by unfinished business. But I also know that we can offer you what you never received—a proper funeral, a release from this torment."

Mohan blinked, surprise flashing across his face. "A funeral?"

The ghost's anger faltered, and for the first time, its voice softened, filled with a deep sorrow. "My body was left in the jungle... torn apart by animals. No one cared enough to look for me, to bury me. I was forgotten. But if my body can be put to rest... maybe, just maybe, I can move on."

Mohan's heart ached as he heard the ghost's words. "We'll find your body, "he promised. "We'll give you the funeral you deserve."

The ghost hovered in silence for a long moment before finally speaking. "If you do this for me, I will forgive you, Mohan. I will leave this world and stop haunting you. But first, you must find my remains."

Mohan nodded, feeling a glimmer of hope.

"Tell us where your body is, and we will make sure you're laid to rest properly."

The ghost drifted closer, its voice heavy with pain. "My remains are scattered in the jungle, near the place of the accident. Some parts were dragged away by animals, but you will find most of me beneath a large banyan tree, deep in the forest."

Mohan turned to the father, his voice trembling with determination. "We have to do this, Father. It's the only way."

The father nodded solemnly. "Yes, Mohan. We must perform the rites and give this spirit peace."

The ghost's form began to fade, its voice barely a whisper as it spoke one last time. "Do this... and I will trouble you no more." And with that, it vanished into the night, leaving only silence in its wake.

Mohan stood there for a moment, stunned by the quiet. He turned to the father, his expression a mixture of exhaustion and resolve. "We'll go to the jungle tomorrow. We'll find the remains and perform the funeral."

The father placed a reassuring hand on Mohan's shoulder. "Yes, my son. Together, we will lay this spirit to rest and free you from its grip. But be prepared, for the journey may not be easy. The ghost's anger has festered for a long time."

Mohan nodded, clutching the cross tightly. "I'm ready, Father. Whatever it takes."

The father gave him a small, encouraging smile. "Have faith, Mohan. Tomorrow, we will bring light to this darkness."

And with that, they turned back to the church, their minds set on the task that awaited them— bringing peace to a restless soul and freeing Mohan from the shadow that had haunted his life for far too long.

As the sun rose the next morning, Mohan and the father stood beside the jeep, the air thick with the weight of what lay ahead. Mohan's face was tense, but there was a new determination in his eyes.

"Are you ready, Mohan?" the father asked, adjusting his robes and clutching his Bible.

Mohan nodded, gripping the steering wheel tightly. "I don't know what we'll face in that jungle, but I'm ready to put an end to this. I owe it to the ghost... and to myself."

The father gave him a reassuring nod before climbing into the passenger seat. "Let us go with faith, my son. The jungle may be treacherous, but we have a higher purpose guiding us."

With a rumble, the jeep roared to life, and they began their journey toward the heart of the jungle. The path ahead grew more and more rugged as they ventured deeper into the dense foliage. The trees loomed overhead, their thick branches casting long, terrible shadows.

"This place..." Mohan muttered, wiping the sweat from his brow as he navigated through the narrow, uneven trail. "It's even more daunting than I remembered."

The father, sensing Mohan's unease, kept his voice calm. "The jungle holds its dangers, but we must trust that we are here for a reason. We are doing the right thing, Mohan."

As they ventured deeper, the jungle grew wilder, more unforgiving. Vines tangled themselves around the jeep's wheels, and fallen logs blocked their path. At one point, they had to abandon the jeep and continue on foot, hacking through thick underbrush.

"I never thought it would be this difficult," Mohan admitted, wiping the sweat from his forehead as he cut through the vines with a machete. "How much farther do you think we have to go?"

The father glanced around, scanning the trees and listening to the sounds of the jungle. "The ghost mentioned a large banyan tree. We must be close now."

They pressed on, the jungle pushing back against them with every step. The thick foliage made it hard to see, and the sounds of distant animals added to the tension. But Mohan and the father kept moving, determined to complete their mission.

Finally, after what felt like hours of struggle, they reached a clearing. At the centre stood an enormous banyan tree, its sprawling roots twisting and curling like the limbs of some ancient beast.

Mohan's breath caught in his throat. "This must be it."

The father nodded. "Yes, I feel it too. This is where the remains lie."

With heavy hearts, they began to search beneath the tree. The ground was uneven, and roots jutted out in every direction, making the task difficult. But after a gruelling search, they found what they were looking for—scattered bones, half-buried in the earth, fragments of clothing tangled among the roots.

Mohan knelt beside the remains, his heart heavy with guilt and sorrow. "This... this is all that's left of him."

The father placed a hand on his shoulder. "We have found him, Mohan. Now we can finally give him the peace he deserves." Together, they carefully gathered the bones, wrapping them in cloth. The sun was beginning to set as they loaded the remains into the jeep and made their way back to the church.

By the time they returned, the sky was a deep, bruised purple, the last rays of sunlight filtering through the trees as they prepared for the funeral rites.

In the quiet of the churchyard, the father began to perform the sacred rites, reciting prayers as he sprinkled holy water over the remains. Mohan stood nearby, his head bowed in reverence.

As the last words of the prayer were spoken, a chill swept through the air, and Mohan felt a familiar presence behind him. He turned, and there it was—the ghost, standing silently, its once-raging spirit now calm and at peace.

The ghost looked at Mohan, its expression softer than before. "Mohan..." it whispered, its voice no longer filled with anger. "I... I am sorry."

Mohan blinked, caught off-guard by the ghost's apology. "Sorry? After everything?" The ghost nodded, a faint glow around its edges. "I was blinded by my pain, my anger. I blamed you for what happened, but in truth, it was not your fault. You tried your best. And now, you have given me the one thing I never had—a proper farewell."

Mohan felt a lump form in his throat as he met the ghost's eyes. "I never wanted this for you. I didn't know... I didn't realize the pain I caused."

The ghost gave a faint smile. "I understand that now. And for what you have done today, I thank you. You have given me peace."

Mohan could only nod, his voice too thick with emotion to speak. The ghost slowly began to fade, its form growing fainter with each passing second. "I forgive you, Mohan," it whispered. "May you find peace as well."

And with that, the ghost disappeared into the night, leaving nothing but a gentle breeze in its wake.

Mohan stood there in silence, feeling a wave of relief wash over him. The weight that had burdened him for so long was finally lifting. He turned to the father, gratitude shining in his eyes.

"Thank you, Father," he said softly. "I don't know how I would have done this without you."

The father smiled warmly, his voice gentle. "You did what needed to be done, Mohan. You faced your past and made peace with it. That is no small feat."

Mohan looked out at the now-quiet churchyard, the final resting place of the ghost. "I feel... lighter. Like a huge burden has been lifted."

The father nodded, placing a hand on Mohan's shoulder. "That is the gift of forgiveness, my son. You have done a great service, not only to the spirit but to yourself."

Mohan smiled faintly, a sense of calm settling over him for the first time in what felt like years. "I think I can finally move on now."

The father gave him a reassuring nod. "And you will, with God's grace. "As they stood in the fading light, Mohan knew that the nightmare was finally over. The ghost had been laid to rest, and with it, the guilt and sorrow that had haunted him for so long. After the ghost was laid to rest and Mohan finally felt a sense of relief, he and the father stood in the quiet churchyard. The night air was calm, but the father's expression was still serious, as if there was more to say.

"Mohan," the father began, his voice heavy with concern, "our work is not yet done. There is one more thing you must take care of."

Mohan, still emotionally drained, turned to the father with a furrowed brow. "What do you mean, Father? The ghost is gone. It's over."

The father shook his head slowly. "No, my son. It's not just about the ghost. The eye of your dog. As long as you keep it, another spirit could find its way to you. You must remove it. Only then will you and your family be truly safe."

Mohan's stomach churned at the thought. "The dog's eye..." he whispered, remembering the terrible feeling he had ever since the accident. He had long suspected that the eye wasn't just any eye, that it held something mysterious.

"Yes," the father continued, "it may have connected you to the supernatural forces. If you don't remove it, you could attract another vengeful spirit."

Mohan took a deep breath, realizing the weight of the situation. "Then I'll do it. I'll get it removed, Father. But I'll need your help with everything—getting my family out of jail, explaining all of this to them... I can't do it alone."

The father nodded solemnly. "Of course, I will help you. We will face this together."

The next few weeks were a whirlwind of legal proceedings. The father stood by Mohan's side, providing spiritual and emotional support, while also working tirelessly to prove that the accusations against Mohan's wife, cousin, and friend were based on false evidence.

It wasn't easy—the legal system required thorough documentation and proof. Mohan had to face interrogations and cross-examinations, reliving the painful events that led to his family's imprisonment.

But with the father's help and the truth finally coming to light, Mohan's family was released from jail. They were confused and hurt, still reeling from the ordeal, but the father gathered them all together in the church to explain the entire story.

"This was not Mohan's doing," the father said as he addressed Mohan's wife Geetha, his cousin Ramesh, and his close friend.

"You were all victims of a much darker force. The ghost that haunted Mohan fed him lies and deceit, twisting reality and making him believe that you all conspired against him. But the truth has come out, and Mohan has paid dearly for believing in the wrong thing."

Mohan, standing quietly beside the father, looked down, guilt still gnawing at him. "I don't know if you can forgive me," he said softly, "but I've done everything I can to make it right."

Geetha stepped forward, her eyes filled with emotion. "Mohan... we've all been through so much pain. But now that we know the truth, we can finally let go of the anger. You were misled. You've suffered just as we have."

Ramesh nodded in agreement, placing a hand on Mohan's shoulder. "We forgive you, Mohan. We're family. We'll rebuild what we lost."

Mohan's heart swelled with gratitude, and for the first time in months, he allowed himself to smile. His family was whole again.

Soon after, with the help of the father, Mohan arranged to have the dog's eye removed in a highly secured hospital. The surgery was delicate, and a human donor's eye was procured for the transplant. The hospital staff was briefed about the nature of the dog's eye, and the father ensured they understood its potential danger.

As the operation proceeded, Mohan lay on the hospital bed, nervous but resolute. The surgeons worked with precision, and after hours of careful effort, the cursed dog's eye was removed, and the new human eye was successfully transplanted.

When Mohan woke up, the father was sitting beside him, smiling gently. "It was successful," the father said, patting Mohan's hand. "You're free from that burden now."

Mohan blinked, adjusting to the new sensation in his eye. "I can't believe it's finally over," he whispered, relief washing over him.

The father leaned in closer, his expression serious once again. "I've warned the hospital staff. The dog's eye must be kept under strict security. If anything were to happen, the consequences could be severe."

For a time, life returned to normal. Mohan received a transfer to another city, and he moved there with his wife and family, ready to start a new chapter. The air in their new home was lighter, free from the tension and fear that had plagued them for so long.

They were finally happy, finally at peace.

But one night, as they sat together enjoying a quiet evening, the phone rang. Mohan's heart sank when he recognized the number—it was the hospital. He answered quickly, his voice tense. "Hello?" The voice on the other end was urgent, panicked. "Mr Mohan, this is the hospital. I'm afraid we have some bad news. The... the dog's eye... it's missing."

(Another story of the dog's eye begins)…